SUMMER LOVIN'

by

J. Sterling

SUMMER LOVIN'
Copyright © 2022 by J. Sterling
All rights reserved.

Edited by:
Jovana Shirley
www.unforeseenediting.com

Cover Design by:
Michelle Preast
www.Michelle-Preast.com
www.facebook.com/IndieBookCovers

License Notes

ISBN-13: 978-1-945042-45-4

Please visit the author's website
www.j-sterling.com
to find out where additional versions may be purchased.

Other Books by J. Sterling

Bitter Rivals – an enemies to lovers romance

Dear Heart, I Hate You

10 Years Later – A Second Chance Romance

In Dreams – a new adult college romance

Chance Encounters – a coming of age story

THE GAME SERIES

The Perfect Game – Book One

The Game Changer – Book Two

The Sweetest Game – Book Three

The Other Game (Dean Carter) – Book Four

THE PLAYBOY SERIAL

Avoiding the Playboy – Episode #1

Resisting the Playboy – Episode #2

Wanting the Playboy – Episode #3

THE CELEBRITY SERIES

Seeing Stars – Madison & Walker

Breaking Stars – Paige & Tatum

Losing Stars – Quinn & Ryson

THE FISHER BROTHERS SERIES

No Bad Days – a New Adult, Second Chance Romance

Guy Hater – an Emotional Love Story

Adios Pantalones – a Single Mom Romance

Happy Ending

THE BOYS OF BASEBALL

(THE NEXT GENERATION OF FULLTON STATE BASEBALL

PLAYERS):

The Ninth Inning – Cole Anders

Behind the Plate – Chance Carter

Safe at First – Mac Davies

FUN FOR THE HOLIDAYS

(A COLLECTION OF STAND-ALONE NOVELS WITH HOLIDAY-

BASED THEMES)

Kissing my Co-Worker

Dumped for Valentine's

My Week with the Prince

Spring's Second Chance

Summer Lovin'

Falling for the Boss

I DON'T DATE CLIENTS

SUMMER

S TARING AT THE folder on my desk, I sorted through the paperwork, reading his name for the hundredth time in bold lettering on the top. *Crew Maxwell.* He was my latest client, due to walk through my office door any moment now. For some reason, I was anxious. And I was never anxious when meeting for a new job. Always professional, unaffected by fame, I was damn good at what I did.

When I was only twenty, I'd started my career as a personal assistant for celebrities before deciding that having my entire life revolve around someone else's wasn't all that appealing. My time never belonged to me. My own existence was always on the back burner, forced to take a seat and be quiet. So, when my best friend and real estate goddess, Seline, told me about a pro baseball player who needed help getting his life in order once he relocated here after being traded, I agreed to help him.

But only temporarily.

I'd learned pretty quickly that professional athletes were given basic information from the front office once they were sent to a new team, but other than that, they were completely on their own. There was no one dedicated to helping them find a place to live or get them situated in any way other than maybe a plane ticket and, if they were lucky, a hotel reservation.

If the guy had a wife or a girlfriend, that kind of thing fell onto her shoulders. And even then, the women sometimes tended to be too overwhelmed to even know where to start. For the single guys, they had absolutely no help. And if they were traded in the middle of a season, they also had no time.

That was where I came in—Summer Brady, short-term relocation specialist for professional athletes.

I'd been doing this exclusively for the past five years. I had yet to hire any staff because, truthfully, I'd been too scared to choose the wrong person and have it all blow up in my face. Basically meaning, I needed to impose a *no falling for or sleeping with the client* rule and have it actually stick.

Some of these guys were relentless, not used to taking no for an answer, and could be ridiculously charming. Not to mention the fact that just their profession alone made them incredibly alluring. Anyone who worked for me needed to be able to resist them on a daily basis. As long as I was a corporation of one, my actions, my behavior, and my ability to stick to my guns when all I wanted to do was drop my damn panties and get fucked on the floor sometimes was all within my control.

That wasn't to say I'd never been tempted or I hadn't almost stopped my new business before it even began when I slept with that anonymous pro baseball player I first helped. He had been constant in his pursuit of me, flirting nonstop, and eventually convinced me that he meant all the pretty things that he'd been saying. Obviously, there was a part of me that enjoyed being wanted by him, and I actually saw us having a future together. And once our contract ended, like a fool, I slept with him.

And never heard from him again.

I had been slightly devastated.

But I was nothing if not a quick learner.

My business, my reputation, and my success were more important to me than getting dicked by a pro baller. And I meant that in more ways than one. A lot of the professional athletes that I'd met over the years were cocky, arrogant, cheating pricks. I witnessed firsthand how they played the women in their lives, and I vowed to never become a fool for one ... *again.*

Professional athletes could not be trusted. It was basically my motto, the only way I'd survived in this business for as long as I had. And even though Crew Maxwell was supposedly still single at the ripe old age of twenty-nine, had never been married, hadn't fathered any children—that anyone knew about—he definitely wasn't innocent. Crew had a reputation for being a player on and off the field. Typical, right? A habitual dater, he always had a woman on his arm. That man was never alone.

Until now.

Recently traded to LA's football team, he was set to be our new starting quarterback in the fall. A trade that had taken everyone by complete surprise, myself included. No one had even remotely suspected that the team was planning on getting rid of our current QB, so when it was announced, it sent the front office scrambling and the local press into a frenzy. Apparently, no one had been tipped off, which was almost unheard of in this industry and this town.

Snitches were everywhere, scooping stories before they were set to go public, always one step ahead. It was hard to keep a secret in LA, but the Crew Maxwell trade was one for the books. I hadn't been prepared for it. For him, his reputation, and what I assumed would be a nightmare job to work on as soon as the team called and let me know they'd given him my contact information. Crew struck me as the type of guy who was used to getting what he wanted, no matter what it was. I wondered for a moment if anyone had ever told him no.

No sooner did the question enter my mind than the six-foot-four tanned god knocked on the side of my door before stepping inside. He was wearing jeans and a black T-shirt that hugged the curves of his muscles, accentuating every single one of them. His dirt-brown hair was tucked neatly behind a backward baseball cap, and I wanted to ask him if he knew what a backward hat did to a woman, but I knew instinctively that he did. Crew knew exactly what he was doing and just how to do it. I tried to pull it together but got distracted by the deep shade of green of his eyes.

I had known the man was sexy. I'd seen him all over the tabloids and in that *People* magazine's Sexiest Man Alive edition, but it was nothing like seeing him up close and in person.

Good God, life wasn't fair. No one should look that good without a filter.

"Summer?" he asked, his Southern accent filling the room as he said my name.

I hadn't expected it—the accent—and it made me grin for a second and forget all about the kind of guy I thought he was. He sounded so innocent.

I pushed to a stand, straightened my pencil skirt, and stepped toward him, hand extended. He took it, and electricity didn't pulse through me, but heat did. Hot desire filled my entire being in an instant, waking me right up with that touch, as if asking if we were finally going to get laid in this century or not.

"Crew. It's nice to meet you. Can I get you something to drink?" I offered, and he shook his head.

"I'm okay," he said before walking over toward my desk and sitting down in one of the chairs.

He was bigger than life, sucking all of the air out of the room simply by existing in it. It was suffocating and exhilarating, all at the same time.

I walked back to my chair and sat down, pulling at his file once more. "Welcome to Los Angeles. And to the team," I said with a smile.

"Thanks," he said, his tone smooth, his grin cocky. "Please tell me that you come with my signing package."

I swallowed hard as his comment slammed me right back into reality instead of whatever sex-deprived fantasy I had been about to get lost in. It was a pretty standard come-on. One I'd heard more than once before. It was like these guys had a manual for hitting on women; they all said the same shit.

"I'm not for sale," was the only comeback I could think of because, technically, I did sort of come with his package, but I wasn't going to admit that. At least, not out loud.

"Never said I wanted to buy you, Duchess."

"Duchess? Really?" I groaned. I would not be able to work like this with him if he was going to act this way. We'd never accomplish anything. "Turn off the charm for two seconds, so we can get through this," I insisted, and the smirk that appeared on his gorgeous face was downright devilish.

He put a hand in the air. "I'll stop. I mean, I'll try, but damn, Summer, have you looked in a fucking mirror lately?" he asked, and I swore my vagina just screamed his name from between my legs. "You can't blame a guy for shooting his shot."

I actually started laughing out loud because that was something I hadn't heard. "That was shooting your shot? Weak, at best."

He leaned back in the chair, still grinning like the damn Cheshire Cat from *Alice in Wonderland*. "Challenge accepted. I'll do better next time."

I started to argue but decided there was no point. Crew was the type of guy who would go tit for tat and had to have the last word. If we began this pissing match, we'd never end it until one of us was underneath the other, getting fucked.

I could think of worse things …

"Okay, so I'm basically your temporary personal assistant. My job is to get you settled and help you with anything that you need. That includes finding you somewhere to live, among other things."

Crew was currently staying in an uber-fancy suite, but he couldn't live there full-time during the season. That was usually the most difficult part of the relocation process—finding housing that worked and made sense. Even with my multitude of contacts, it could still be an issue, depending on whether they wanted to buy or rent. Los Angeles was a huge city, and most guys didn't want to drive two hours each way to get to the field, but if they had a family and kids, it changed everything.

"Ah." He looked into my eyes and held them with a firm stare. "So, you do come with the package."

Dammit. I knew he'd call it out.

"Short-term," I tried to insist but couldn't stop smiling.

He was annoying but charmingly so. And so … fucking … hot.

"How long is short-term?" he asked, his face pulling

together as he waited for me to respond.

"I can work with you for a maximum of two months, but anything after that, we'd have to hire you some permanent help."

"Who else do you work for in these two months?" He leaned forward, his elbows on the edge of my desk as he watched me with those dark green eyes.

"Just you."

"So, you're exclusive to me then?" he pushed, and I felt my entire body tingle.

"I mean, I guess you could say that."

"A lot can happen in two months, Summer."

"Yeah, like we can find you someplace to live. Get your new life settled and into a routine that works best. So much can happen," I said, trying my best to stay focused and get us back on track, and he just laughed.

"Like me getting you into bed and tasting every inch of that fucking perfect-looking body. That can happen within two months too. Shit, that can happen every single day for the next two months."

Okaaaay.

No one had ever been so forward before. At least, not

this quickly. His hand disappeared to where I couldn't see it, but I knew that he was adjusting his cock underneath his pants. That meant that he was hard. This man, who had walked into my office all of three minutes ago, was hard for me. I shouldn't have been turned on, but I was.

Part of me had wanted to strip out of my clothes and hop into his lap the moment the words left his mouth, but I held strong and convinced myself that I was only feeling that way because I hadn't been properly fucked in months. The last time was a bad blind date that Seline had arranged, which only ended up in bed because I needed to dust off the cobwebs from my poor, unused girl.

Looking back at the experience, I should have left them there.

"I don't date my clients. Sorry."

"Never?" he pressed.

I could tell that he wanted to know if I'd ever broken the rule before. I had, only that one time, but I wasn't about to admit that to him. I barely knew the guy; I sure as hell didn't trust him.

"Never," I said, the lie flowing easily and convincingly from my lips.

"Well, technically, I won't be your client after sixty days."

On any other day, it would have been a good point, but per usual, I'd heard that line before. I wondered briefly how annoyed he'd be if I told him that he needed some new material. See, I'd heard it all. Every technicality, every loophole, every way that a man could attempt to get a woman into bed—it had all met my ears in some form over the years.

I eventually learned that it was the challenge more than anything else for these guys. I was forbidden fruit, so to speak. Someone they were told they couldn't have. Men, athletes especially, were competitive creatures. Dangle the carrot in front of them, and they'd not only chase it, but also devour it the second it was in their grip.

All I had to do was remember the way things had unfolded in the past and see that we were following a similar timeline. Most of my clients disappeared pretty quickly after our time together was up. That was how I knew that it hadn't ever been real for them in the first place regardless of how convincing they might have been to the contrary.

Nothing they'd said was true. It couldn't have been. Because one after the other, they all followed the same pattern of walking away, taking their pursuit of me with them. Any other woman might have had a breakdown over it, taken it personally, or wondered what the hell was wrong with them.

But not me. I'd caught on pretty quickly that it was about the sex and little else. The way these men acted had nothing to do with me. It was about them and their dicks. They weren't looking for a relationship or anything serious, even when they'd initially proclaimed to be. I was a game, and they not only wanted to play, but they wanted to win as well.

"You're not my type," I lied once again because Crew Maxwell was the type for every woman with eyes. He was a freaking god. An Adonis. And I bet he fucked like one too.

"Let me guess." He pressed a finger against his full lips. "You don't date football players."

"I don't date professional athletes. Hard rule," I said, but my tone was all kinds of contradiction.

It had come out sounding like I was flirting, and hell,

maybe I was. But I didn't flirt with my clients. This was why it was so much easier when they had a girlfriend or a wife. I worked directly with them instead. No mixed signals. No lines crossed. No flirting. End of story.

"Rules are meant to be broken, Duchess," he said, calling me that hideous nickname again. "And I like breaking them."

"God, you're so arrogant." The words slipped out of my mouth before I could even think about not saying them.

I hated the bravado that most guys hid behind, refusing to show their true selves to anyone, but for some annoying reason, it worked on Crew. Being confident was one thing, but arrogance and cockiness were other beasts altogether, and he wore them all in spades like a superhero.

"I'm sure you'll find plenty of women in LA who would be happy to give you whatever you need. The town's practically known for it."

Cleat chasers. Groupies. Puck bunnies. Jersey chasers. Fans.

LA was filled with them. People wanting to do whatever it took to land a guy with money or to further their career. And I wasn't only referring to the women here. The men in this town behaved in this way too. It wasn't a gender thing, but more of a Hollywood industry thing. Whatever it took to get ahead, people were willing to do it.

Crew leaned forward, his arms hitting my desk and staying there as he blew out a soft breath, those dark green eyes meeting mine. "I am arrogant. But I've earned it. And you like it. Now, what do you need from me, Duchess?"

Gah!

This man was going to challenge me at every turn, and I hated how much I was enjoying it. I needed to remind myself that he was exactly like every other guy who had ever stepped foot in this office before him. Crew Maxwell was no different than the rest. He wanted one thing, and once our time was up, he'd go away, just like all the rest had.

THIS MIGHT WORK OUT IN MY FAVOR

CREW

I WAS NOT deterred by anything that came out of Summer's luscious mouth. I didn't believe half the things she was trying to sell me on anyway. And she knew it. Summer had to be tough, untouchable, professional. And I wanted to fuck it all out of her. Every last bit of armor she hid behind until she was lying bare beneath me, screaming my name.

I was watching her—staring really, but she was downright mesmerizing, and I was entranced. Like some voodoo priestess out on the Louisiana bayou, where I had grown up, I swore Summer had put some sort of spell on me. Little did she know, she didn't need it.

I'd wanted her riding my cock the second I laid eyes

on her. She was exactly my type—tall, long-legged, beautiful, smart, independent, and sassy with a mouth that needed to be punished. I knew, verbally, she wanted to give me a run for my money, but she held back every time she got worked up enough to start. I let it go because there was plenty of time for me to wear her down.

Two months, to be exact.

Honestly, LA giving me Summer was the best thing they could have done. I was grateful that she was going to help me because I had no idea how to navigate this place. The city was paralyzing. It moved too fast. Was far too crowded, spread out, and didn't make any sense geographically. I wasn't sure I was going to like anything about being here, except my paycheck.

And maybe the pussy.

But that had never been an issue. Not even back in high school, where my star had first started rising. Girls had been throwing themselves at me for as long as I could remember. And once it started, it never stopped. Not that I took them all up on the offer, obviously. I'd actually been doing it less and less over the past few years, only going out with women that I hoped would lead somewhere. Not that you'd know it by the things you read in the press. It always amazed me how easily it was to lie online. Cite an "anonymous source," and an entire article filled with bullshit became believable.

Not that I usually cared. None of them were truly defaming, and thankfully, no one had accused me of anything unsavory. But my reputation as being the biggest player in the game always seemed to precede me, and I could tell that Summer was all too aware of it. I'd change her mind soon enough.

"I'm going to ask you a few questions to get started."

I watched as Summer gripped her strawberry-blonde hair with both hands and twisted it quickly before it became a knot, sitting perfectly on top of her head.

Fuck.

I wanted to undo it, pull it, and wrap it in my fingers while I fucked her from behind until it all unspooled and spilled down her back.

"How'd you do that?" I asked, fascinated by women's tricks, and she laughed.

"What?"

"Your hair." I stared hard before shaking my head.

I watched as her cheeks turned red, and she pretended not to be affected by me as she grabbed a pen and pulled out a notebook. She wanted me just as badly as I wanted her, but she had to act like she didn't. It wasn't professional to want to fuck your clientele until you couldn't see straight.

"Did you bring a car?" she asked, completely ignoring my question about her hair and moving into work mode.

"No. I left it back in Louisiana. Figured it was easier," I said because the trade had happened so fast that I didn't even have time to think, let alone make definitive plans for my things. One day, I had been at home, and the next, I had been on a plane, headed for training camp in Los Angeles with my new team.

"I get that. You'll need a car here though. You have to drive in LA. So, I can either arrange to have your car shipped out or we can get you something new. It's up to you," she said.

For the first time since I'd signed my new deal, I felt relieved instead of guilty about my paycheck.

No matter what team I played for, I consistently took less money so that we could build a better team overall.

No one could ever look at my salary and say that I was the reason we sucked or had a losing season. The sheer amount of injuries we'd kept having the past two years was the reason for that. I wasn't to blame, which was why this trade had been so surprising. Honestly, it felt like it had come out of nowhere. Me and the old LA quarterback had basically been swapped for one another.

To me, it made no sense. But it didn't have to. Football was a business, and I was simply a player. I either went along with it or I got the fuck out. And I was still in my prime, so I wasn't going anywhere.

"Let's just get something here," I suggested, and she scribbled down some notes.

"Okay. I'll need you to email me a list of car preferences or types that you're interested in, and I'll arrange a private showing. That should be first on our list so that you can get to and from training and the stadium."

"All right. Easy enough," I said because I already knew exactly what I wanted. A metal-gray G-Wagon, fully tinted, decked out with all the bells and whistles.

There were two things I insisted on being an unreasonable prick about—my car and my home. I worked hard and deserved to have a little luxury in my life, so I splurged on those two things and very little else.

"Do you have any idea what you'd like to do in terms of housing?"

"What do you mean?"

"Do you want to rent something, or do you want to look into buying property?" She waited for me to respond, her blue eyes watching my every move as I contemplated my answer.

I'd actually thought about that a little on the plane ride over, but every time I tried to research it online, I got overwhelmed, said fuck it, and slammed my laptop shut.

"I have a dog," I started to explain, and her whole face lit up like I'd just told her I rescued fifty kittens on the freeway this morning.

"What kind of dog?"

"He's a big, fat yellow Lab."

"Is he here already?"

"Yep," I said, popping the *P*.

I'd bought him a seat in first class with me, and the two of us had flown over in style.

"He needs a yard." I couldn't imagine keeping Bart in

an apartment or someplace where he couldn't get out during the day if he needed to. Which was exactly our current situation, considering that we were living in a hotel suite.

Summer started scribbling again on her notepad. "Okay. So, I think we should look at houses then, so he won't be cooped up all day with nowhere to go. Unless you're planning on hiring a dog walker, which I definitely recommend for the times when you're on the road or will begone at the field."

"Yeah. I had someone help me with Bart before. I'll probably need that out here too," I said, and she continued her quick writing.

"I can help you find the right person. For the housing, rent or buy is probably the biggest question."

Leaning back into the chair, I folded my arms across my chest. I had more money than one person needed, but it felt like I could absolutely blow through it all in this town if I wasn't smart or cautious.

"What do you recommend? Do you have any thoughts?"

She laughed, and I wanted to bottle the sound up and

take it home with me, where I could jerk off to it later.

"I have lots of thoughts."

Is she flirting?

"Any on housing?" I asked, playing it cool.

"Yes. Here's the thing. What we would need for you, in terms of a rental, is going to cost a lot each month. I'm talking in the thousands, depending on the location and size of the home. It makes more sense to purchase something, honestly. Real estate is usually a good investment. Especially out here. And I have a great agent I work with who won't dick us around."

I felt my possessive streak flare to life. "What agent?"

"My best friend, Seline," she said, and the flare died out on the spot. "She is a great resource, super knowledgeable, and won't steer us wrong."

Summer had said *us* instead of *you*, and the caveman inside of me wanted to pound my damn chest, proclaiming that I'd won the girl when I hadn't even started yet.

"I think I'd like to buy something, but I can't stay in this hotel for the next month with Bart. Is there somewhere else I can rent in the meantime while we look?"

"Yes, I can find you something," she said, writing on

her pad again.

"Summer?"

"Uh-huh?" she mumbled, still focused on the paper in front of her instead of on me, where I wanted her attention.

"What if I'm only here for a year?" It was a rare moment of brutal honesty that I couldn't help but spit out.

The question had been floating around in my head since I'd first learned of the trade. Even though I'd signed a multiyear contract, that didn't mean shit in the overall scheme of things. My old contract hadn't meant anything; otherwise, I'd still be there.

She stopped writing and lifted her head to look at me. "Then, we can rent your place out, or we can sell it. It would take a lot for you to lose money on the purchase. But, Crew"—her eyes softened—"it's not going to be just one year, okay?"

"Sure," I said before pulling it together and remembering who the fuck I was. "You'll help me look and stuff? I don't have the kind of time to—"

"I know. That's why I'm here. I'm all yours for the next two months. I won't leave you hanging."

"Promise?" I asked, forcing her to tell me she'd stick

around as long as I needed her, desperate to hear her deliver the words so I could hold her to them.

"Promise," she agreed, and I was momentarily satisfied.

HE WAS GOING TO BE A HARD ONE

(That's What She Said)

SUMMER

W E WRAPPED UP our initial conversation by exchanging phone numbers and email addresses. The second Crew walked out of my office, I swore he took all the air with him. I sat in my chair, staring at my computer screen, my brain in some sort of hot Crew fog. The man had temporarily broken me. And his moment of vulnerability hadn't helped.

It made no sense because every single athlete I'd worked for in the past was incredibly sexy, but Crew was on another level. Hell, he was on another damn planet.

My phone pinged, and I glanced at it, seeing Seline's

name on the screen.

Pressing the text button, I read her message.

"How was it?" was all she asked, and instead of even trying to respond with words, I called her instead.

"Ooh, so good you had to call?" she teased, her soft French accent infiltrating through the line.

"I'm sitting here at a complete loss for words. I need to pull it together," I admitted, and she laughed and clapped at the same time.

"Are you flustered? I've never heard you like this before."

"Tell me about it. I'm …" I stuttered. "I don't know what I am."

She breathed into the line, and I pulled the phone away from my ear before putting it back. "Okay, Summer. Focus. Does he need a house?"

That worked. I snapped out of whatever spell Crew had put on me and went straight into work mode. "Yes. He needs a house, and we want to buy instead of rent. He has a dog. But let me talk to him about potential locations first. We didn't even get that far."

"What the hell did you even discuss then?"

I growled into the line, feeling frustrated because Seline knew as well as anyone that those first meetings could be super overwhelming, especially when the new location was unfamiliar territory. "It was an introduction. Basic needs and light conversation only. Just to get us started."

"Well, I'm going to send you a list of where his childless teammates live, so you have some sort of jumping off point. You find out all the particulars—how many rooms, budget. Unless you want me to contact him directly," she suggested, and I ground my teeth together in response, thankful she couldn't see me.

"Seliiiine." I dragged out her name even though she knew that wasn't how this worked.

I was the middle person for a reason. There was no direct contact between the vendor and the athlete. The fewer people who had access to the player, the better. I handled all potential issues that arose and put out fires before Crew ever knew they'd sparked to life. That was my job.

"Just teasing. Ooh, this one's gonna be fun," she said before saying, "*Au revoir*" and ending the call.

I knew that her brain was already going a mile a minute, and before I even had the chance to send her a list of potential neighborhoods, she'd be sending me one instead.

I opened up my email on the computer and started constructing one to send to Crew, telling him that it was nice to meet him today and that I was looking forward to working together before reminding him to give me a list of cars he was interested in so that I could set up a showing.

Even though we were currently only working on two items, both were big tickets and could take a lot longer than two months if I didn't do my job well or if Crew's demands were too particular. It was better to get started on what I hoped would be the easier of the two as soon as possible. Guys were happier when they had a car that they loved.

THREE HOURS FLEW by before I knew it, and I'd found a handful of furnished rentals with a yard for Bart. When I pulled up my email to send Crew a list, I saw that he had responded to my initial car request. His email was short and concise, and I hated that he hadn't even flirted a little.

Why was I like this with him?

There was no signature or sign-off at the end, just one sentence describing exactly what he wanted. Crew was precise. A little too precise, and I wasn't sure the dealership would have one available, but I started emailing my contacts to ask anyway before crafting my own non-flirtatious email in return.

My cell phone rang the second I pressed Send, and I looked down at it, seeing Crew's name flashing on the screen.

"Did you get my email?"

"I did. I can't work like this," he said, and I wanted to laugh at the tone of his voice. He was trying to be friendly, but I could tell he was frustrated.

"Like what exactly?"

"I can't do all of this over email. I need to print things out and see them in real time. That's how my brain works. I need visuals and not on a screen."

He sounded like he was almost embarrassed even though there was absolutely no reason for it. All of us processed things differently, and it made sense to me that he liked seeing things the way he did for football—most likely hand-drawn charts on pieces of paper.

"I can do that. Do you want me to come by the hotel?" I offered because that was what my job was—to show up wherever my client was at, work closely with them, and make their life easier.

"Please. That would be really helpful. Clothing optional," he said, and I barked out a laugh into the line.

"Had to go there, didn't you?"

"Couldn't resist."

"Can we do this tomorrow? Will that work?" I asked and waited for him to answer. When he didn't, I pulled the phone from my ear to make sure our call hadn't been disconnected. "Crew?"

"I'm here."

"Tomorrow okay?" I asked, sensing that he was going to tell me no.

"Tonight would be better."

I could argue or tell him that I had plans, but I didn't. I simply responded with, "See you in twenty," before ending the call and pulling up all the links I'd sent him in the email and printing them out.

There was no sense in fighting with Crew. Especially when I knew I wouldn't be on the winning side. I worked for him and only him—a point I'd made very clear in our meeting earlier. That meant that I was basically at his beck and call, and he knew it. Although if he ever worded it that way, I'd probably knee him in the nuts.

Grabbing a manila folder, I stuffed the information on the temporary rentals in there along with a map of the counties. Right as I was about to head out, I got a response from one of my car guys, letting me know he had *the* car. I printed that email out as well, fired back an acknowledgment, and asked him to hold it for the night.

DAMN GOOD AT HER JOB

CREW

I SAT IN my ridiculously oversize suite chair after showering, stared at Bart, and waited for Summer to arrive.

"Be nice to her when she gets here." I pointed at my fat Lab, his ears perking up at the sound of my voice.

He gave me a low growl, and I narrowed my eyes.

"Just don't jump on her. And no slobbering."

Bart barked, so I took it as him agreeing with my demands even though we both knew that he'd do whatever he wanted the second she walked through the door anyway.

I'd never had him trained. Bart wasn't a bad dog by any means; he was just easily excited and liked to knock people on their asses. Not that I'd mind if Summer fell on her ass. I mean, I could be her knight in shining armor that way. Carry her from the floor and right into the bedroom, where I'd feast on her until she forgave my dog and forgot her own damn name.

"Never mind, buddy. Jump all you want," I said right as someone knocked on the door three times.

Bart started barking as he ran to the source of the sound, blocking me from even getting to it.

"Guard your loins, Duchess," I yelled, and she complained from the other side as I shoved Bart with my knee to get him out of the way.

Bart busted through the small opening I'd created and did exactly what I'd known he'd do. He knocked Summer right on her perfect ass. Papers spilled all over the floor, and I ran to her, apologizing, but she wasn't even remotely pissed. She was laughing, grabbing Bart's fat head and kissing him on his nose.

My dog was getting more action from this woman than I was. He was going to have to go.

"You didn't tell me he was so cute," she said through her giggles as Bart licked her face.

Summer wiped it away, her blue eyes searching over

my dog's fat head to find mine. I extended a hand toward her, and she took it. I effortlessly pulled her up, like she weighed nothing—because I was strong, dammit, and manly, and tough.

"Sorry for this knucklehead," I said as I grabbed Bart by the collar and shoved him inside the room before shutting the door.

"It's okay. I don't have a dog, and I miss it," she said almost wistfully as we both bent down and started gathering up the papers that he'd scattered. "Thanks."

I handed her a fistful, and she shoved them back into a folder before standing up and straightening her skirt, which was now filled with blond dog hair.

Pulling the key card from my back pocket, I swiped it against the door and pushed it open, holding it for her to walk through first, my eyes glued to her ass before she turned around and caught me.

"Crew," she pretended to scold, but I sensed somewhere deep down that she either liked or appreciated it.

"You can't blame me, Summer. It's a fantastic ass," I practically growled, hoping my dick wouldn't get too hard.

"You're incorrigible," she said, but there was a grin on her face.

Once we were both inside, she stopped moving, her hand resting on Bart's head as she waited for me to take the lead.

"Let's go over things at the table," I directed, and she was off again, switching back into business mode.

"Okay, these are the currently available furnished rentals that I emailed you. This is a map of the neighborhoods." She pushed a picture toward me. "I circled the stadium and the training camp facility in blue. I also wrote how far each city was from both at the bottom there." She pointed toward her perfect penmanship at the lower end of the map. She had written the number of miles and also how long my commute would be.

"All of these places take dogs and are move-in ready?" I asked, studying the map like I had any fucking idea what it all meant. I wasn't familiar with any of the actual cities in Los Angeles County or Orange County.

"Yes. I've already contacted people at each place and told them our situation. They're all waiting for my call once we decide. Oh shit," she said before slapping her hand over her mouth. "Sorry."

"Don't apologize for swearing. It's hot." I gave her a wink, and she shook her head like she was tired of my shenanigans.

"I found the car."

"Already?" I felt my pulse start to race as the little boy in me who was obsessed with nice cars started jumping up and down inside my body.

"Yeah. Want to go see it?"

"Hell yes!" I shouted, and Bart barked.

"Perfect. We can talk about the housing while I drive us there," she suggested before giving Bart a pouty look. "Will he be okay if we leave him alone?"

I looked at my fat-headed Lab and gave him a pat. "He'll be okay. Won't you, boy?" I directed the last question toward Bart, who suddenly looked sad, like he knew I was heading out again.

"Oh my God, Crew. Look at his face. He knows we're leaving." She sounded heartbroken. "How do you leave him every day? I can't take it, and I just met him."

I watched as she dropped to her knees and wrapped her arms around his thick neck, hugging him and not even caring how much hair was getting all over her clothes. I glanced down at my dick, willing it to behave because every single thing this woman did made me hard. It was ridiculous. She was a walking boner-giver.

Pulling Summer to her feet, I stopped myself from yanking her straight into my arms and kissing her fuckable mouth. "Stop trying to steal my girl," I admonished Bart instead as he wagged his tail at the two of us.

"Don't listen to him," Summer said to my dog, bending over and giving him a kiss on the nose. "I'm not his girl."

"Stop doing things that make me want to punish you, Summer," I warned, and she let out a gruff sound.

"Get over yourself, QB-One," she said, rolling her eyes. "This isn't happening." She wagged a finger between our two bodies, and she was damn lucky I didn't grab the thing and start sucking on it before sticking it inside her, so she could feel how wet I made her.

I took a menacing step toward her, so she would hear me loud and clear. "There's attraction, and then there's whatever this is between us," I started to say. "I'm not sure it even has a name. You can try to fight it all you want, but

I'll have you know that I always win, Duchess."

She stepped back in response. "Except last season, right? Isn't that why you're here in the first place?"

Ouch.

Fuck.

"That was mean. I'm so sorry," she immediately apologized, and I knew that she meant it. "It's just that what you're saying and doing, Crew, I hear it all the time. Every single athlete I work for thinks he feels the way you do," she explained, but I'd stopped listening after "every single athlete."

Just the thought of another man thinking that he could have her made me crazy. I wanted to break things, punch walls, throw shit through windows. It didn't matter that we'd just met. I hadn't been lying when I said that there was attraction and then there was whatever this was. This wasn't something as simple as chemistry between two people. I'd experienced that a thousand times before. I was familiar with what lust or wanting to fuck someone and never see them again felt like.

This. Wasn't. That.

"I'll let it go," I growled. "For now."

"Oh gee, thanks. How big of you," she said.

I stopped myself from saying something snarky in response. Yes, it took a lot of self-control, thanks for wondering.

ONCE I WAS in the passenger seat of her Range Rover Sport, I opened the folder I'd grabbed before we headed out of the room and started looking at the printouts. I was thankful that Summer hadn't given me twenty options to choose from. It was like she had known that would be way too many. There were only five, but each one was located in a different city that meant nothing to me.

"If you were picking one of these, which one would you choose?" I asked because it seemed like the easiest way to at least start up the conversation.

Marina del Rey meant as much to me as Manhattan Beach did. Cool names, but I had no clue where they were or what they were like.

Summer glanced at me briefly, her eyes moving from my face to my shoulder, and I watched as she inhaled a little too quickly. Yeah, she liked what she saw. I was going to have to be shirtless the next time she came over.

"That's a tough question." She paused before answering, "But I think I'd choose one of the beaches— Manhattan or Hermosa. It's a little more laid-back than the other cities, and a lot of professional athletes already live in the area and actually have a life there, so it's not like you'd feel like a prisoner, if that makes any sense." She turned her head to look over her shoulder as she flicked the blinker and changed lanes, making her way toward the upcoming exit.

"Meaning that I could go out and not get mobbed?" I asked because that was definitely a difficult thing to do regardless of where I lived.

"In theory," she said. "I mean, tourists might bother you. But most of the locals wouldn't."

"Manhattan or Hermosa," I said as I picked up the two options for each city and tossed the other three onto the floor of her car.

Summer gave me a look as we stopped at a red light at the bottom of the exit. "My car is not a trash can."

"I'll pick them up. I just need simplicity," I said. It was true though. The less clutter my brain had to focus on, the better. I needed things simple, to the point, and obstacle-free. It was how I functioned the best. On and off the field.

"We're here," she said.

I looked up from the papers and out my window as we pulled into a Mercedes dealership, but instead of using the normal entrance, Summer continued driving toward the back before stopping her car near the service exit.

"Can we look at both of these properties?" I asked, and she nodded.

"I'll set it up for tomorrow. Email me your practice schedule, so I can work around it."

"Okay," I agreed before asking, "Will we have any houses to look at in that area too? To buy, I mean?" I didn't want to start living somewhere and get comfortable there, only to pack up and move somewhere else six weeks later.

"Oh, absolutely. I can definitely set that up if you like it enough. But let's wait until we see these rental places in person. That way, you can check out the community and see if it's your vibe or not." She waved her hand in the air, and I stopped myself from laughing at her use of the word *vibe*. "Don't give me that look," she scolded, as if reading my mind. "You might not like the area. Maybe it will be too crowded, or feel too small, or too beachy," she added, and this time, I did laugh.

"Is there such a thing as too beachy?" I asked because I had no fucking idea what that even meant.

"When you're not a pro surfer, there can be. The beaches are a big draw here in SoCal, so they get crowded, and neither Manhattan or Hermosa is really that big of a city. So, they can get pretty jammed up really quickly."

"Gotcha," I said even though everywhere I'd been so far in Los Angeles felt jammed up. Nothing was easy to get to. Everything took a fucking hour and a half, even when it was only twenty miles away.

But I'd never lived by the ocean, and it sounded like a damn dream. If I was going to live in Los Angeles, I might as well do it right.

HOUSE-HUNTING

SUMMER

I PICKED CREW up two days later in my car and did everything I could not to stare at his massive frame sitting in my passenger seat the entire time, like I'd done the other night. His broad shoulders were a work of art, but I refrained from telling him that—or drooling. Most guys in his position were slim while still managing to be strong, but I wouldn't describe Crew that way at all. He was one of the more muscular quarterbacks I'd ever met.

"How's the G-Wagon?" I asked as soon as I pulled out of the hotel parking lot, referring to the gorgeous car he'd ended up buying.

The look on his face when he'd sat inside of it was downright adorable. For once, he didn't look like a professional football player or the starting quarterback for

LA's team, who was used to getting everything handed to him.

No.

Crew Maxwell had looked like an excited guy who couldn't believe he was not only getting to drive the expensive car, but also take it home with him.

"It drives like butter. Bart loves it," he said, and I giggled.

"You already took Bart for a ride?"

"Right when I got home. Fucking thing's already full of his hair, but whatever." He waved it off like it was no big deal.

"You could have brought him with us today, you know," I said because this house was as much for Bart as it was for Crew.

"Really? Do you think I should have?" Crew shifted in his seat, and I considered turning around.

Shrugging my shoulders, I gave him a look. "I mean, he needs to love the house too, right?"

"Shit," he mumbled, and I knew what I needed to do. Putting my blinker on, I made a U-turn at the next light. "What are you doing?"

"Going to get the new love of my life," I said matter-of-factly. "You'll run upstairs and get him while I fold the seats down."

"You're a fucking dream," Crew said, and I pretended like it didn't matter. Like I hadn't heard compliments like that a thousand times before. Because I had. From every single athlete who had come before him.

No matter how much I wanted to believe him, I reminded myself that I couldn't. That believing the words coming out of his mouth would only lead to heartbreak—mine.

I stopped in front of the hotel entrance and worked on folding the seats down. They didn't go all the way flat, but it would have to do. Hopefully, Bart would be okay and not slide all around as I drove and took turns. Before I knew it, both of the guys were downstairs, one of them wagging his tail excitedly at the sight of me.

I leaned down and rubbed his head. "I feel the same way, buddy."

I was starting to get attached … to the dog.

"Why don't you greet me like that?" Crew complained as he lifted his giant dog into the back of my Range Rover.

"Bart doesn't want to sleep with me and never talk to me again," I blurted out, wishing I could take it back as I moved into the driver's seat to get away from my words, which now lingered in the air between us.

Crew slammed the back door, hopped into the passenger side once more, and wrapped the seat belt around that too-sexy frame before reaching out and touching my hand with his. "You think I want to sleep with you and never talk to you again?"

Dragging my hand out of his grip, I ignored the question, put the car in drive, rolled down all of the windows a bit so Bart could stick his head out, and started toward Manhattan Beach. His question wasn't something I wanted to get into. He'd deny it, of course. They all had.

He'd try to convince me how it wouldn't be just a one-time thing or how he wasn't like the other guys I'd worked with and how he would never treat me that way. All things that I'd heard before over the years. Just usually not this fast. I was afraid if Crew started pushing now and didn't stop that I'd eventually give in. And for some reason, I just knew instinctively that it would hurt a hell of a lot more to learn that it wasn't real for Crew than it ever had with that baseball player.

So, I changed the subject. "I told you that Seline, my real estate agent and friend, was meeting us there, right?" I asked even though I knew that I had.

Seline was already waiting at the rental property. She'd sent me a text a few minutes ago. She wanted to get a feel for what Crew's taste was and talk to him a little about what he was looking for in a purchase home. Mostly, I thought she just wanted to meet him in person. I didn't give her enough information about him every time she asked, and she was nothing if not impatient.

"Yeah. Why is that again?"

"She wants to see your reaction to the place, I think. It helps her match you to your dream home. She's incredibly good at what she does," I said, talking Seline up even though it was all the truth.

Seline had some crazy natural gut instincts, which allowed her to never come off as pushy, and she seemed to know what would be a good fit for her client way before they ever figured it out on their own. It was part of the reason why she sold more houses than anyone I knew and without doing a single ounce of marketing. All of her business came from word of mouth and referrals.

"Manhattan Beach first, right?"

"Yes," I said, not spilling the fact that I lived pretty close by and had basically driven back and forth this morning to get him.

When our working relationship came to an end and everything he thought he felt for me went back to normal, my being that close to his living quarters might be an uncomfortable thing. So, I kept that detail close to the vest. There was no reason for him to know that information anyway. If we happened to run into each other at some point down the road, I was sure it would be like whenever I ran into any of my other previous clients … who had a gorgeous female by his side.

So, why does that thought make me so sick to my stomach?

As we neared the first house, I felt myself growing a little nervous. Seline was absolutely stunning. The type of woman I could see Crew with. And she was single. What if he liked her? Or even worse, what if she liked him?

"Are you okay?" Crew's voice broke through my thoughts, and I turned to glance at him quickly.

"Yeah. Why?"

"You were making that face," he said, as if he knew all of my faces already when there was zero chance of that being possible.

"What face was that?" I pushed, anxious to hear his interpretation.

"The overthinking, *worried about something* face," he explained like he'd seen the expression a million times.

I was pissed that he'd nailed it right on the head when he should have been far off, at best.

"I'm not. I wasn't," I stuttered, and he grinned. My flustered response proved to him that he was right.

"I'm not going to be into your friend, Summer. And I don't give a shit if she's into me," he said, and I wondered if I'd said all of my previous thoughts out loud or not. That would make perfect sense as to how he could have *read my expression.* "You did talk out loud, by the way."

Dammit. That's what I get for talking to myself in the car all the time. I don't even realize when I'm saying all my thoughts out loud anymore.

I slowed my car down and came to a complete stop in front of an iron gate. Punching in the code, I waited for it to swing open before pulling all the way in and coming to a stop. "I don't care if you're into her. She's gorgeous," I said, lying through my teeth because for some reason, I did care. I cared a whole hell of a lot.

"So are you."

Two quick raps on the passenger window had Crew turning to see Seline's magazine-worthy face staring back at him. Bart started barking from the backseat, and Seline's face twisted as she peered behind Crew.

"Did you bring a dog?"

I opened my door and slid out, waving Seline over to my side of the car and away from Crew.

"Holy hell, Sum. He's stunning," she whispered in my ear as we hugged.

"Trust me, I know."

"Is he following suit?" she asked.

I knew exactly what she was referring to—*Is Crew doing what all the other guys have done previously?*

Nodding, I raised my eyebrows and answered, "Like a damn user's manual."

"Unfortunate." She tsked, sounding far more disappointed than I'd ever allow myself to be.

"Tell me about it."

HOT WOMEN TRAVEL IN PACKS

CREW

SUMMER WAS RIGHT. Her best friend, Seline, was fucking gorgeous. She looked like she belonged on the cover of every magazine, no Photoshop or airbrush needed—her face was that flawless. But I'd seen a million gorgeous women, and for the most part, they acted exactly the same. Most wanted the perks that went along with dating a professional athlete, hoped for a ring, and prayed even harder for a kid. The "accidental" pregnancy was the meal ticket.

It hadn't taken me very long to realize that beautiful women had been told their whole lives that they were beautiful and nothing else, so it became the one thing that defined them. Outside of their looks, most of them had no idea who else they could be or why they should even try. A lot of the women I'd met never actually worked a day in their life and had things handed to them simply because they were pretty.

Tell someone something so many times, and they started to believe it.

Kind of like me with football. Who was I outside of being a quarterback? I wasn't always sure, if I was being honest with myself.

Which was why meeting someone like Summer had knocked me off my feet from the get-go. She had the looks to be like every other female, but she wasn't. She worked hard, had made a name for herself, was praised for the career she'd built from scratch and celebrated for it as well. Hell yes, I'd stalked her social media profiles and all of the press I could find on her the other day. I'd almost thrown a fucking party when I didn't see her pictured with any men online.

I'd heard Summer when she told me that every guy had said all these things to her before, but I didn't care because I knew myself well enough to know that I meant them. I wanted to fuck her so hard that she'd never walk right again, but it was more than that. If I were only looking for a woman to stick my dick in, I could find that anywhere.

Summer was the total package—looks and brains. Not to mention the fact that she might love my dog more than I did. Speaking of, she was currently holding on to him with one hand while she juggled her keys, purse, and paperwork in the other.

Jogging toward her, I reached for all of her things instead of Bart and watched as both women threw each other a look I wished like hell I could interpret. Sometimes, women spoke their own language, and it wasn't for anyone else.

"You look cute, holding Summer's purse, Crew," Seline fired at me, her accent permeating every word.

"I'm secure enough in my masculinity to handle it," I fired back, and she laughed while Summer stood there, shaking her head.

"Where are you from, Seline?" I asked and noticed Summer's expression falter slightly. She thought I was doing exactly what I'd sworn I wouldn't do in the car—fall for her friend.

"I grew up in a small town in France, but I've been here for years. Just can't seem to shake the accent completely," she said with a wicked grin that I knew made most men weep. But not me. I'd only be weeping for the strawberry-blonde with blue eyes, currently holding my dog.

"I've never been to France," I said because I'd done very little traveling outside of the United States, no matter how many times people insisted that I make the effort. It always felt like I had no time to go anywhere and truly enjoy it. The last thing I wanted to do when I went to Europe was to be rushed and not even get to see anything. "Have you, Summer?"

She shook her head. "No. I've been to London a handful of times but not France yet."

"We'll go together then," I said with a shrug, and Seline nudged her with her elbow.

"Yeah, yeah. Let's go look at the house." Summer redirected our attention to business, just like she always seemed to do. "Are you excited to see the backyard?" Summer asked, and when I turned to answer, I realized ee that she was talking to my dog and not me.

"Stop making me jealous of my fucking dog," I complained, and Summer stuck out her bottom lip and pretended to pout.

"Aww, poor tough guy. I'm sure your ego can handle it," she said as she wrapped Bart's leash around her hand and held him tight as she walked through the gate in the backyard instead of the front door.

"You obviously don't know me very well," I grumbled under my breath, and Seline was next to me in a flash.

"She doesn't trust you," she whispered.

I pretended like I hadn't just heard that, so I wouldn't draw Summer's attention. If she noticed me and Seline talking between ourselves, she'd convince herself that we were flirting, doing exactly what she feared, and I didn't want to play into any of that. I might be an asshole sometimes, but I hated emotional games. Football excluded.

"I didn't even do anything," I complained quietly, hoping Summer wouldn't notice.

"You're doing what every other man has done since she took this job," she explained even though Summer had told me the exact same thing already.

"Yeah, she mentioned that."

I watched as Summer unhooked Bart's leash from his collar, and he took off running in the oversize space before he dropped to his back and started rolling around on the perfectly manicured lawn.

"I think he likes it," Summer shouted, the smile on her face a fucking joy to behold—literally. She filled me with happiness, just from watching her.

"Listen, Crew"—Seline grabbed my shoulders and turned me to face her straight on—"the other guys just wanted to screw her. I saw it in their eyes, no matter what other pretty words came out of their mouths. They were all full of shit. But you seem different." She narrowed her brown irises at me and pursed her plump lips together. "I think you might genuinely be interested in our girl here."

"That's what I'm trying to tell you both," I argued, and she put her finger to my lips to shut me up.

"She'll never believe you. Not until your work with her is completed. Because this is what happens every time," she started to explain, and before I could even ask her what happened every time, she was telling me. "They all act like they want to be with her. But the second their contract is up and Summer is done working for them, they disappear and go away like she never existed. That's why she knows it's not real. She learned pretty quickly that people get caught up in their emotions while they're in certain situations. When she's the only businesswoman you're around, you think you love her. But when she's out of sight, it all ends."

"If you two are finished flirting, we have a house to see." Summer's annoyed tone broke through the insightful information Seline had been giving me, and instead of being upset for the interruption, I swiveled in Summer's direction.

"We're not flirting, Duchess. I only flirt with you."

"Uh-huh," was Summer's response as I started walking toward her and the open glass back door.

The backyard of this rental was perfect for Bart; I almost didn't care what the inside looked like. It was only temporary anyway.

"See? She doesn't believe a single word coming out of your mouth. And she won't. Unless you're still around, annoying her, after her contract with you is up."

"I get it, Seline. Thanks for the tip." I hadn't meant to

come off so short with her, but I understood what she was telling me. It was something that I'd already picked up on.

I'd try to cut back on all the crap Summer had heard a million times before and make sure that when our contract expired, I was still standing there, waiting for her to give me a shot.

And I wouldn't be taking no for an answer.

I'M IN TROUBLE

SUMMER

WE DIDN'T EVEN visit the other house in Hermosa. Crew insisted that there was no need to look any further. He loved the Manhattan Beach rental, the neighborhood, and when I drove him around the small downtown to check out the restaurants, bars, and the pier, I thought he audibly moaned the second the ocean came into view.

I tried to tell him that Hermosa was a little less "bougie" and had a more laid-back, party atmosphere, but he simply shook his head and told me we were good.

"Tell them we want this place. I asked Seline to pull properties here as well."

"Are you sure?" I asked because things weren't always as glamorous as they seemed at first.

"Why? Should I not?"

I sucked in a breath. "I was just thinking that you should see what it's like to actually live here for a minute before you buy property. I mean, what if you end up hating it?"

"You think I will?"

"I honestly don't know. I just err on the side of caution, is all," I tried to explain because I'd hate for him to buy something and then decide that Manhattan was too busy, or too far from the field, or not for him.

"Okay." He nodded his head. "Okay. Put a pin in Seline, and I'll see how I feel on a day-to-day basis first. That's probably the smart thing to do, right?"

"I think so. I mean, do you have any concerns at all?" I asked as I slowed down behind the car in front of me.

"Only the traffic. It seems really crowded here. And I hate the idea of not being able to go anywhere."

I understood what he was saying. The beach cities during the summer were absolutely packed, so he was currently seeing it at its worst. Not to mention the fact that the streets were small and narrow with homes packed along both sides, causing cars to bottleneck easily. It was honestly kind of a pain in the ass to live here.

"It's summer, so it's the worst time, but everywhere in LA is kind of like this. As long as we get you a couple blocks away from the sand, you'll have an easier time, getting in and out."

"Speaking of," he said, his face suddenly all lit up, "is there one close by?"

I scrunched my face together before I realized what he was asking. "Oh, an In-N-Out? Like burgers?"

"Yes. I'm dying to try one."

Laughing, I asked, "You've still never had one?"

"Nope. Be my first." He placed his hand on top of mine, and I pulled it out from his grip … again.

"You have to stop doing that," I squeaked out because his touch was like a freaking magnet. I wanted to chase it every time it left me.

"I can't," he said before Bart made his way toward the front of the car and put his head between us on the console. "Hey, buddy."

"There's one not too far from here, but there will be a line."

"Is there never not a line?"

"No."

"Take me there, Duchess."

I tried to stop the smile, but it spread across my face anyway. "Fine. But only because I don't want to hurt Bart's feelings and he needs to experience it as well."

We drove in relative silence, to my surprise, down Highway 1 and toward a random In-N-Out location I'd pulled up on my Maps app. This man was lucky I loved their food; otherwise, I might have put up a fight. Ah, who the heck was I kidding? I would do whatever he asked.

I mean, I did work for him after all.

It's part of my job description, I thought, lying to myself.

We were currently parked in the lot, our food sitting in cardboard trays on our respective laps. I grabbed a fistful of freshly made fries and shoved them in my mouth before sharing some with Bart, who was drooling on my floormats, his tail wagging excitedly.

"Are you going to take a bite or stare at it all day?" I teased, waiting for Crew to inhale the burger like I wanted to do. But I refused to stop watching him, and eating my own burger would distract my attention. I couldn't remember a time when I'd been present for someone's first taste of In-N-Out, and I wasn't going to squander the opportunity to see the reaction firsthand.

"I'm feeling pressured," he whined, and I smacked his shoulder with my hand, pretending not to notice how hard his arm was. "What if I hate it?"

"I don't care if you hate it. I don't own the place."

"If you pull out your phone and start filming, I'm getting out of this car and walking home," he said from behind his sunglasses, but it was an empty threat. There was zero chance he'd make Bart walk all the way back to the hotel.

"I'm not going to film you, but now, I kind of want to." I stopped talking for a second before adding, "I mean, think of the marketing. You could be in their next commercial." I wasn't sure I'd even seen an In-N-Out commercial before.

He wrapped his hands around the burger and started slowly moving it toward his mouth. "Okay. I'm going in."

I watched as he took the world's biggest bite before chewing, his head nodding the entire time like he was having some sort of secret conversation with himself.

Holding my breath, I waited for him to say something ... anything ... so I knew whether or not to surprise him with the food sometime in the future

"You're killing me," I complained. "Come on, Crew. Do you like it? Hate it? Think it's overrated? What?"

He started smiling before a gruff laugh slipped out. God, he was gorgeous. I hated how attracted I was to him because I knew his so-called attraction was only temporary.

"You make torturing you so much fun."

I growled, and he laughed again.

"See?"

He took another bite of the burger, the secret sauce dripping onto his chin, and I had to forcibly stop myself from reaching out with my tongue and licking it off.

What the hell is wrong with me?

"This burger"—he finished chewing—"is definitely not overrated. It's like the perfect combination of ingredients. The hot burger with the crisp lettuce. Whatever this sauce is, it's fucking delicious."

"And you haven't even tried the fries yet," I said, now sounding like I did own the place, as pride coursed through me.

It was a California thing.

He reached for the shake I'd forced him to get and slurped it through the straw, making me grin. "Why is everything here so good?"

"Fresh ingredients. Real milk for the shakes. Real potatoes for the fries. Nothing's ever frozen. Apparently, that makes a difference," I fired off the reasons like us Californian's had been born with them in our blood or something.

"How soon do you think we can move in?" he asked, and I blinked a few times to refocus.

"I'll call the listing agent when we get back to the hotel," I said because I didn't want to make the phone call while we were in the car. Whenever I handled business on the phone, I needed the space and privacy to wander around. Sometimes, I ended up down the street from my house without even thinking about it.

"Sounds good."

We both finished off our food, and I started the engine before heading back toward Crew's hotel to drop him and Bart off. I was running through the list of what I needed to get done in my head—call the listing agent, see how quickly Crew could move in, find a dog walker, make sure the security cameras on the property were in working order, make a list of local numbers and resources for Crew to access easily, call Seline and put her house-hunting on pause.

"Where'd you go?" Crew's voice broke through my inner thoughts.

"Work," I answered easily.

"But I'm your only job, and I'm sitting right here. I demand your attention."

Shaking my head, I didn't even turn to look at him as I responded, "You have it, Your Highness."

"I just like it when you're paying attention to me."

"Crew, seriously, what do you want from me?" This time, I did turn to glance at him. It was going to be the longest two months of my life if he acted like this every single time we were together.

His expression twisted before a cocky, know-it-all grin replaced it, and I forced myself to look away. I wasn't sure if he was going to be honest or spoon-feed me a line of crap and expect me to swallow it.

"Just your heart, your soul, and that smoking hot body to twist and turn at my every whim," he said without taking a breath.

I glanced at him again, extremely annoyed. "Can you be serious for two seconds?"

"I am being serious."

"Mmhmm," I said, forcing myself to focus on the road.

LA traffic was no joke, and I'd be pissed if I crashed my car. I loved my car. And those feelings were real—unlike the ones Crew kept spewing out at me.

He wanted to have sex with me.

How fucking original.

BART, THE ULTIMATE WINGMAN

CREW

COULD I HAVE been any more typical in my response to Summer's question? No, I couldn't have. I was a fucking idiot who had just promised her best friend that I'd back off until our contract was over so that she'd realize that I actually meant what I was saying.

But, dammit, I was a fool when it came to this woman. She'd asked a question, and I hadn't wanted to lie. What I'd said was the truth. I wanted it all when it came to Summer, and apparently, I needed her to understand that.

There was no way in hell I'd be able to last two whole months without knowing what she tasted like. Those lips were meant to be on mine. That body had been made for my hands. I was going to have to figure out a way to get her to give in. Because sixty fucking days was fifty-nine too long.

When she pulled into the main entrance of my hotel, I took my time in unbuckling my seat belt and getting out of the car, trying to think of something clever to say to make her stay longer. "Do you want to call the listing agent from my room?"

She gave me a look, those blue eyes judging me. "It's okay. I have some other things I need to handle, so I'll be in touch as soon as I've worked out the logistics. To be clear, you'd like to move in as soon as possible, yes?"

"Yes, and—shit." I just remembered something I'd been meaning to tell her all day before I got distracted by her existence.

"What?"

"I'm leaving town for two weeks."

"What? When? Why?" Her tone sounded more like a questioning girlfriend than whatever it was that she was supposed to be for me.

"Coach scheduled a group-training-slash-bonding-trip for the team."

"The whole team?"

"The starting offense," I corrected.

"So, you'll be gone for two weeks?" She actually sounded upset.

"Is that okay, Duchess?"

She rolled her eyes. "Stop with the nickname already. Of course it's okay, but I need the details. You'll need someone to watch Bart."

How could I have forgotten about him?

"We leave in a few days," I said. "Friday. Can you watch him? I'll pay you extra. Whatever you want. I just can't think about leaving him with a stranger, and he already loves you." I was piling it on extra thick, but it felt necessary.

Summer shifted in her seat, turning around to face Bart but not saying anything.

"I'll be gone, so it's not like I'll need anything. And you said you only work for me, right? Is your home dog friendly?"

She reached for Bart, petted his head, and ruffled his face with a grin. "I'll watch him. Now, get out. I have a lot of work to do in a limited amount of time."

I did as she'd asked. And Bart and I stood there,

watching her drive away before some kid ran up and asked me if I was *the* Crew Maxwell. Then, he took a selfie with me before disappearing and coming back with his mom, who did the same.

"I'm staying here, too, if you want to get drinks or something one night." She wagged her eyebrows at me, and I knew exactly what she was offering.

My eyes roved the length of her body without meaning to, and she flicked her hair in response. It was honestly a habit to check people out. I did it with men as well. Not because I wanted to fuck them, but because it was in my nature.

"I'm in training. Sorry." I tried to be polite, but I was annoyed on the inside.

"Are you sure? I can come to your room after I put Jonathan to bed. Anytime. I'm here for a week," she babbled on, sounding desperate as she tried to touch my arm but I moved out of the way.

I didn't even say a word before turning my back to her and walking toward the elevators, giving the security guard a nod as I pressed the button and the doors opened.

"Ma'am, you're going to have to take the next one,"

the security guard said when she tried to squeeze inside with me and Bart.

"But it's empty. Surely, Crew Maxwell can share his elevator like a gentleman."

"Hotel policy. You can take the next one," he said again, sounding stern.

I stopped the smile that wanted to spread across my face as the doors closed, locking me away from her. I made a mental note to slip that guy a little cash for helping me out.

My phone started ringing, and I wondered who it could be before seeing Summer's name on the screen.

"Miss me already?" I answered, and she made some sort of annoyed huff. "Gotta stop with those sounds, Summer. You know what they do to me."

"Crew, pay attention," she demanded.

The elevator dinged before the doors opened, and thankfully, no mom was waiting on the other side. I half-suspected the mom from downstairs might have run up to beat me here.

"Hold on one sec. Let me get into my room and let Bart off his leash."

"Okay," she said, sounding agreeable.

Bart wagged his tail as we walked down the hallway toward our door. I unhooked the leash from his collar, and he ran inside the room, heading straight for his bowl of water and making a mess all over the floor. I wondered if I should warn Summer that he was messy in everything that he did but thought better of it. Bart could be messy. I was clean. She'd love me more.

"Crew?"

"Yeah, I'm here. Sorry. What's up?"

"I talked to the agent for the house, and she said you could go ahead and start moving in today if you wanted."

"Seriously?" I asked as I took in the state of my room, thankful that I hadn't really unpacked any of my things for this reason exactly.

"Yeah. I told her you were under a time crunch. She'd already run your credit and approved you, so she was basically waiting on you to say yes. Do you want me to head back over to the hotel and start loading up your things?"

"I knew you missed me," I breathed into the line, and it went quiet.

Pulling it away from my face, I looked at the screen, which was now showing my new team logo as the screen saver. She'd hung up on me. I guessed I deserved it.

"Buddy, she's coming back," I said in Bart's direction, and he barked, the water dripping off his face rolls. "We gotta get our shit in order."

I rushed around the room, tossing all of my bathroom shit into a travel bag before grabbing the piles of dirty clothes all over the floor and shoving them into a duffel. I'd be ready to go by the time Summer arrived, so we didn't waste any time. When I emptied out Bart's water bowl, he whined, confused, before I told him that it would be okay. I put all of his food and treats in a separate pile, stacked his bowls into each other, and did one last sweep of the room to make sure nothing that mattered was being left behind.

The sooner I could get checked out of this place, the better. It wasn't that the hotel was bad by any means, but I did enough hotel living during the regular season to last me a lifetime. I needed a home. And Bart needed a backyard.

The knock on the door let me know Summer had

arrived already. She must not have gotten too far when the agent told her we could move in. When I opened it, she stood there with her hand on her hip, scrolling through something on her phone. Bart practically knocked me over the second he realized it was her.

"You're my favorite male," she whispered against his head, and I made a silent vow to change that.

TWO WEEKS WITHOUT CREW

SUMMER

I HELPED MOVE Crew and Bart into the rental house that afternoon. It went a lot smoother than I'd expected it to. But that was because underneath it all, Crew was a pretty simple guy. He never asked for much and was easy to please. Which was saying a lot because most athletes were kind of little bitches, honestly, who whined, complained, and were rarely satisfied.

Bart and I drove Crew to the airport a couple days later, dropping him off for his team-bonding trip like we were some kind of couple. When he got out of my car, he stared at me for too long, and I half-wondered if he was going to lean in and give me a kiss good-bye. I thought I would kiss him back if he did, which was definitely a problem. Instead, Crew reached back for Bart and told him to be good before grabbing his duffel bag and disappearing into the terminal.

I watched him walk away and stayed a little longer after the doors closed, for no damn good reason at all.

Seline had told me the other night that I was in trouble with this one, and I'd refused to acknowledge the truth in her statement, no matter how hard she pushed. I fired off a text to her, demanding that she come over after she was done working. With Crew gone, I really didn't have much to do, but I figured that we could gather a few home options for him to consider once he got back. That was, if he still liked living in Manhattan Beach.

"I guess it's just you and me," I said to Bart as I pulled out into oncoming traffic.

It had been so long since I'd had a dog to take care of, but Bart was so damn lovable that I knew I was going to dread giving him back when I had to.

Maybe Crew will let me keep him, I thought to myself before giggling. No one just gave their dog away.

Later that afternoon, my phone pinged with a text message as I sat on the couch, waiting for Seline to finally get here. I rubbed Bart's head, who was hogging up the whole thing.

> CREW: SEND ME A PICTURE OF YOU AND BART. I MISS YOU
> GUYS.
>
> ME: WHO IS THIS?
>
> CREW: *PICTURE OF MAD FACE*

The picture was super hot and sexy and made me actually ache between my thighs.

> ME: *PICTURE OF BART ONLY*
>
> CREW: YOU'RE BAD AT FOLLOWING DIRECTIONS.
>
> ME: I COULD SAY THE SAME THING ABOUT YOU.
>
> CREW: WANT TO SPANK ME?
>
> ME: CREW.
>
> CREW: SO, THAT'S A NO?
>
> ME: YOU'RE INFURIATING.
>
> CREW: SO, YOU'RE SAYING I SHOULD BE PUNISHED THEN?
>
> ME: ...
>
> CREW: LOL. I'LL STOP.
>
> ME: ...
>
> CREW: SUMMER.
>
> ME: CREW.

CREW: ...

ME: HOW ARE THINGS GOING WITH THE TEAM?

CREW: ARE YOU SURE YOU WANT TO ASK ME THAT?

ME: WHY WOULDN'T I?

CREW: YOU MIGHT GIVE ME THE WRONG IMPRESSION. YOU KNOW, LIKE YOU CARE ABOUT ME OR SOMETHING.

ME: I CARE ABOUT THE MENTAL STATE OF MY CLIENT. NEED TO KNOW WHAT TO EXPECT WHEN HE GETS BACK INTO TOWN.

CREW: IS THAT ALL?

ME: WHAT OTHER REASON COULD THERE BE?

CREW: YOU'RE FALLING FOR ME. YOU MISS ME LIKE I MISS YOU. YOU LOOOOVE ME. YOU WANT TO HAVE TEN THOUSAND OF MY LITTLE FOOTBALL BABIES.

ME: I'M NO LONGER RESPONDING TO YOUR TEXTS.

CREW: *SILLY FACE EMOJI* YES, YOU ARE.

ME: GOTTA GO. SUPER BUSY.

SELINE FINALLY SHOWED up after I took Bart for a walk and checked on Crew's house, just to make sure everything was okay. She arrived with Thai food in hand, so I couldn't be too mad at her. Mostly, I was just bored. I didn't sit around and do nothing very well. It wasn't my strong suit.

"Sorry I'm late. This client made me take him to three houses he'd already seen four times before. He keeps visiting the same ones, claiming that one will speak to him."

"If he doesn't feel spoken to by now," I started to give my two cents when she put a hand up.

"No. I mean, really speaks to him. Like he hears voices in the home."

"Like dead-people voices?"

"I didn't get that far. I just nodded along and told him to let me know but that we couldn't keep visiting houses we weren't planning on making offers on." She groaned. "Luckily, in this market, they'll all be under contract soon enough, and we won't be able to go back in." She dropped down in a chair at my table and started pulling items out of the bags. "The commission on whatever finally speaks to him is going to make me sing."

Walking into my kitchen, I pulled out two plates before joining her at the table, undoing the takeout cartons one at a time. Bart followed me, never more than two steps behind. When I sat down at the table, he lay at my feet, his giant Lab head looking up at me like he was starving even though he'd just eaten.

"Your job is insane," I said, reaching for a set of chopsticks and breaking them apart. Rubbing the two sticks against each other, I watched as the single splintered piece ground itself down to nothing.

"I know. But it's not always like this," she said before adding, "Got to get it while the getting's good."

I'd known Seline since she'd started in the real estate market, and I'd seen her make more money in a month than I made in a year. I'd also witnessed the flip side as well. There were times when she'd go months without a single sale. Which was why she was never frivolous with her earnings. Seline saved and bought nice things but never got herself in over her head.

"How's lover boy?" she asked after taking a bite of her food and swallowing it.

"Who?" I played dumb, and she pointed toward the table with her chopsticks.

"I brought over a few property listings not on the market yet that I thought he might like. But I know you

told him to press pause until he's been here a little while."
She stopped stabbing the air, and I nodded as I reached for
them.

"I'll take them. I'm sure he'll like it here, but I want it
to be his decision, you know?" I explained like I always
did. "I don't want him to feel like he has no options and is
only doing what I suggest."

"Does he know you live literally three blocks away?"
she asked with a grin.

I shook my head. "No. And you're not telling him
either."

"Where does he think Bart is?"

"At my place."

"Which is where?"

"I didn't say."

"And he didn't ask?"

"Nope."

"He's never asked you where you live?" she
questioned.

I realized that it was sort of weird that he'd never
wondered. Most guys asked. But then again, Crew didn't
know where anything was out here, so what would be the

point?

"No."

"Don't you think that's odd?" Her accent grew a little stronger, and I straightened my back in my chair.

"I didn't. But now, I do."

"Anyway"—she waved me off—"I am going to tell you something, and you're going to listen." She gently ran her hands across the napkin in her lap before folding them in prayer pose on top of the table between us.

"Seline, don't." I tried to stop her because I knew she was going to tell me that Crew was different or something of that nature, and I wasn't sure that I could take hearing it from her as well. My heart was already hoping that he wouldn't be like all the rest, but it was too soon to be hopeful.

"I think he really likes you," she informed me. "There. I said it."

"He might. Today," I argued, but she already knew what was coming next.

Seline was the one who had experienced it all with me. She was the person who had picked me up after I fell apart from the baseball player. The one I made a pinkie promise with that I'd never fall for the lies again. Seline was who I told all of the pick-up lines to, relayed all the things I'd heard from the athletes I worked with, and then was just as shocked as I was when they disappeared as quickly as they'd appeared. It made me feel marginally better to know that I wasn't stupid to think they'd meant what they said. Seline said she would have too. She'd met most of them and seen the way they acted.

"It's safe to say, he's not like the rest."

"We can't possibly know that. Not until it ends." To stop myself from talking more, I focused on my plate and continued eating.

She blew out a breath like she was annoyed with me when, if anything, she should have been completely understanding. "Which is why I told him that exact thing," she said.

I dropped my chopsticks to the table, flicking pieces of rice all over. Bart scooted toward the mess, his tail wagging as he greedily cleaned up the remnants of food from my floor.

"You what?"

"Don't get mad at me. I told him that if he was truly

into you, he'd prove it when your contract ended," she finished with a shrug. "What's the big deal?"

I had no idea what the big deal was, truly, but I felt betrayed, angered, irritated. "I don't know. But now, he can just play whatever game he's playing for longer—until I fall for it and give in."

"Summer, he's not going to do that. I see the way he looks at you."

"Like I'm a meal he can't have," I reminded her because all men liked a challenge. They lived for being told they couldn't have something and then proving everyone wrong.

"No. He looks at you like a meal he doesn't want anyone else to have. Like he'd kill them if they even thought about touching you. He watches you like he's in awe of you. Protective. Like he'd jump in front of a fucking bullet to keep you safe. It's not a challenge for him. I can spot those guys a mile away now. And so can you."

I swallowed hard, my eyes watering slightly with her words, so I sucked in a long breath and quickly wiped my eyes before any moisture fell. It had been such a long time since I'd let a man get emotionally close to me, and Crew had started crossing the line the day he walked into my office.

"I know you've been hurt in the past. And a lot of these guys do nothing but lie to you to try to get in your pants. We deal with that shit on a daily basis, being women. But I really don't believe that Crew just wants your"—she started looking around the table before grinning—"fortune cookie, and that's it."

"My fortune cookie?" I giggled.

"It sounded classier than saying *your pussy*," she said, and we both winced for no good reason.

Seline's phone started vibrating across the table, and I watched as she chased it with her hand before grabbing it and rolling her eyes at the screen before answering.

When she pushed up from the table, I knew that she'd be leaving soon. Seline worked at all hours, no matter what.

Looking down at Bart, I petted his head, rubbing that spot between his ears. "Wanna go for another walk?" I said, and he hopped up instantly, his tail wagging. The sun would be setting soon, and the beach was gorgeous this time of night.

"I have to go. I'm sorry." Seline reappeared just as I was hooking Bart's leash up to his collar. "You already knew."

"I know you," I said, giving her a kiss on the cheek. "Thanks for the talk."

"Will you listen?"

I pursed my lips together but didn't respond to her question. She made a loud *argh* sound.

"I figured. But you're just putting off the inevitable. Trust me, this man is not going to give up until you give in."

She was right, and I knew it. Hell, even Bart probably knew it.

When you gave your heart to someone as an adult, it felt different than giving it away as a kid. For whatever reason, it seemed like you had more to lose as a grown-up.

When we were young, we bounced back easier. We tried again. We didn't let love make us quitters. We chased the high, searching for our next Prince Charming, determined that he was looking for us too.

But somewhere along the way, we stopped believing in

fairy tales, in being saved by a knight on a white horse and in happily ever afters. We knew that they existed; we just didn't think they happened to us. Disappointment eventually piled up, leaving us jaded and bitter.

If I gave in to Crew Maxwell, I knew without a single doubt that I was going to fall harder for him than I'd ever fallen for anyone in my life. And that scared the hell out of me because loving like that meant that it could break me even more than I thought possible.

Could people survive shattered hearts?

SEXY TEXTING

SUMMER

S ELINE'S WORDS, EVEN though there hadn't been many of them, repeated inside my head as I lay in bed, Bart taking up the other half. Her message had been loud and clear, and I was starting to believe it more than I wanted to. That small seed of hope was blossoming inside my chest, where it had no right to be.

Why couldn't I just put Crew in a box with all the others and close the lid?

I berated myself for my inability to not have feelings for him. It wasn't just his flirting, the apparent chemistry, or the way he looked at me. It was ... something else entirely that I couldn't quite name or place. I'd be lying to myself if I said this didn't feel different with him. It did.

CREW: ARE YOU AWAKE? I'M SITTING HERE, IN MY ROOM, AND I CAN'T STOP THINKING ABOUT YOU.

ME: YOU MEANT TO SEND THIS TO SOMEONE ELSE, RIGHT?

CREW: NO.

ME: GO AWAY.

CREW: NEVER.

ME: *PICTURE OF BART ON THE BED*

CREW: THAT ISN'T EVEN REMOTELY FAIR.

ME: WHAT ISN'T?

CREW: HE GETS TO BE IN YOUR BED, BUT I DON'T.

ME: HA! HE'S NICER THAN YOU ARE.

CREW: THAT'S NOT TRUE.

ME: HIS ONLY NEGATIVE IS THAT HE SHEDS. DO YOU SHED?

CREW: YES. BUT ONLY WHEN I'M BETWEEN YOUR LEGS AND YOU'RE TEARING MY HAIR OUT WITH YOUR HANDS.

ME: ...

CREW: YOU'RE PICTURING IT NOW, AREN'T YOU? I SURE AS FUCK AM.

ME: CREW.

CREW: ADMIT YOU WANT ME, SUMMER. JUST FUCKING ADMIT IT.

ME: I CAN'T.

CREW: YOU CAN. I KNOW YOU DON'T BELIEVE ME, BUT I FUCKING MISS YOU. YOU'RE THE ONLY PERSON I WANT TO TALK TO AND TELL THINGS TO.

ME: I'M THE ONLY NON-FOOTBALL PERSON YOU KNOW. THAT'S WHY.

CREW: THAT'S NOT WHY. DO YOU MISS ME?

ME: NO.

CREW: LIAR.

ME: FINE. ONLY BECAUSE I'M SUPER BORED. YOU'RE MY ONLY CLIENT, REMEMBER?

CREW: THE TEAM LOVES ME.

ME: ARE YOU SURPRISED?

CREW: A LITTLE.

ME: WHY?

CREW: I DON'T KNOW. I FIGURED THEY WOULDN'T ACCEPT ME SO EASILY. THAT THEY'D HAZE ME OR BE EGOTISTICAL PRICKS. BUT THEY'RE ACTUALLY REALLY NICE.

ME: I'M GLAD YOU'RE MAKING NEW FRIENDS, HONEY. BE A GOOD BOY.

CREW: IF I'M BAD, WILL YOU PUNISH ME?

ME: WHY DO YOU TURN EVERYTHING INTO SEX?

CREW: *HAVE YOU SEEN YOURSELF? GO LOOK IN THE MIRROR. I'LL WAIT.*

WAITING

CREW: *YOU'RE STUNNING. YOU'RE FUCKING GORGEOUS, AND I DREAM ABOUT YOU DAY AND NIGHT. I WON'T APOLOGIZE FOR IT.*

ME: *YOU DREAM ABOUT HAVING SEX WITH ME?*

CREW: *I DREAM ABOUT HAVING A LIFE WITH YOU. AND SEX IS DEFINITELY PART OF THAT LIFE.*

ME: *I HAVE TO GO. I'M WALKING BART. THERE'S A SQUIRREL.*

CREW: *WE'RE NOT DONE WITH THIS CONVERSATION.*

THERE WAS OBVIOUSLY no squirrel, but Crew saying that he dreamed about having a life with me had almost made me drop my phone and Bart's leash. He continued to surprise me, and, God, I wanted to believe the things he said. It was easier for me to dismiss him when all he did was constantly bring up sex. But when he got deeper than that, my heart pounded and raced. I stared at his message one more time before moving to pocket my phone when it suddenly rang.

Glancing down, I saw Crew's name on the screen. I thought about not answering but caved. "Yes?"

"How's the squirrel?" His voice reverberated through the phone, and my knees grew weak. I hadn't realized how much the sound of it affected me or how much I'd missed hearing it.

"Safely in a tree," I lied.

"I'm going out with the guys in a little bit, but I wanted you to know that I'll be calling you later. I want to talk to you."

"What about?"

"Us," he said point-blank, and I stopped moving, holding on to Bart's leash as tight as I could.

"There is no us."

"Not yet. But there will be. When I get back into town, I'm taking you out on a proper date. I'm not waiting for our contract to end. I'd rather die before waiting that long to taste you. I miss you like crazy, Summer. I should be thinking about this damn team and how to win this upcoming season, but all I keep thinking about is how to score the girl who's stolen my heart."

I stood completely still, like everyone within a mile

could hear the things Crew had just said to me. I had no idea what to say in response. My ego urged me to argue, just to make him fight even harder for me, but the rest of me wanted to cave.

"I'll call you tonight," he said before ending the call.

I looked right at Bart, who was staring at me, sitting like a good boy.

"Your dad is very bossy," I said, and he barked.

FORCING THE ISSUE

CREW

THERE WAS NO other way to handle Summer than to be aggressive with her. If I played it cool or too laid-back, she'd leave me in a heartbeat, and I couldn't have that. I had to take the reins and force her into submission. Deep down, I knew she'd love it even if she fought against it at first.

Strong women needed even stronger men.

And I was going to show Summer that what she needed was me.

I was currently at a bar with my teammates. It'd started off nice, empty, pretty much just us and the two bartenders. But word must have spread that we were in town because I watched as it slowly filled up with scantily clad, desperate women on the prowl, all pretending not to see us while they took pictures, using their friends as decoys just to get us in the background. Did women really think we were that stupid?

It didn't matter. I only had eyes for Summer. My mind was on her twenty-four/seven. I hadn't been lying when I told her that. I should be eating, breathing, and dreaming about football and how to win this season, but instead, I was dreaming about eating her. Among other things.

Every time I imagined this upcoming season, I saw her there. When I pictured my future, my home, my life, Summer was part of it all. There wasn't a time when I didn't see her by my side.

So, when an attractive female walked up to me, basically shoving her fake tits in my face, I reared back, making sure she knew I wasn't interested. It didn't deter her as she bent down and asked for a picture, her finger running down my shoulder as I flinched from the unwelcome contact. I offered a halfhearted shrug, and before I knew it, she was sitting on my lap, her arm wrapped around my neck. As soon as the photo was taken, I shoved her off of me.

"I'm not available," I said, and she gave me a trying-too-hard-to-look-sexy grin.

"Neither is half your team, and they're still going to fuck my friends later," she said like she was proud of this fact. Like screwing guys who weren't single was some sort of badge of honor to be displayed proudly on her lapel.

The whole cheating aspect of the game wasn't something that I promoted. Why get married and have kids with someone if you were just going to fuck around in every city we visited? Stay single then. Less people got hurt that way.

Trust me, my opinion on that front was not at all popular. But it didn't change my mind. The only thing I'd learned over the years was to keep my mouth shut about it. What the other guys did had nothing to do with me and wasn't any of my fucking business or concern. But I still thought it was shitty.

"It's not going to happen," I said again, once I realized that she wasn't going away.

"I can rock your world like it's never been rocked before," she said, her tone one hundred percent serious.

I stopped myself from laughing in her face. "I highly doubt that."

"I'm double-jointed." She leaned down once more, telling me that tidbit in my ear, and I pinched the bridge of my nose like her presence was giving me a headache.

"And I have the biggest cock in three counties," I countered with some equally ridiculous shit. "I'm going to ask you to respectfully get the fuck away from me."

Her eyes grew wide, but her forehead didn't even move. "You don't have to be so rude."

"I do because you won't listen."

"Fine. I'll find someone else then."

"Good luck," I said, raising my beer glass toward her as she finally left me alone.

I reached for my phone and sent Summer a text, reminding her that I would be calling later and to not even think about blowing me off. She sent back some smart-ass response, and I told her that if she didn't answer, I'd fly out, and we'd have this conversation in person. She was much more agreeable after that, clearly unsure of what I was capable of doing or not when it came to her.

I was exhausted, anxious, and wanted to call my girl. The rest of my teammates weren't ready to leave and were all grown-ass men, so I didn't give a fuck what they did as long as they showed up for drills in the morning on time and ready to work.

I figured they'd give me a ration of shit about me wanting to bail early, but they were otherwise occupied with Miss Double-Jointed and her friends. I used that to my advantage as I called a car and snuck out alone.

Once I was in my hotel room, I tossed off my hat and jumped onto the bed, phone in hand. I stared at it for a minute, maybe two, trying to plan exactly what to say to Summer. She was going to resist my idea, give me reasons why it was a bad one, and I needed to have a comeback in response.

You don't need a comeback, idiot. You just need to prove it to her with your actions. Your words and your actions have to match.

I pressed her name and watched as the phone connected and started ringing. Summer answered quicker than I'd thought she would. Actually, I figured she'd make me go to voice mail on my first try.

"Hello?" Her voice was flirty, and I could tell she was smiling.

"Hey, Duchess," I said, the nickname naturally sliding

out and without thinking.

"Argh," she groaned through the line, and I laughed.

"Stop acting like you don't like the name, Summer. You like it now. If I stopped calling you it, you'd miss it," I teased, hoping it was the truth.

"Fine. It's grown on me," she admitted before adding, "a little."

"I'll take it," I said as Bart made some sound in the background. "Oh man. I miss him too. Hang on. I'm calling you back."

"Wait, what?" she started to argue, but I'd already ended the call and pressed the video-chat button instead.

"I should have known," she said as Bart's face appeared on the screen.

"Hey, buddy. Do you miss me?" I said, but Bart kept moving in and out of the frame, even as my talking to him grew more frantic.

"I don't know that dogs can see our phone screens. Do you think they can?" Summer asked as her face appeared, and my dick instantly grew hard at the sight of her.

"I think they're more affected by sound and smell maybe," I offered, like I was some sort of Jedi Master on the subject. "God, you're truly beautiful."

Her face disappeared as the phone screen turned black. I heard shuffling sounds, like the speaker was being covered before she reappeared, her lips pressed together in a thin line.

"Everything okay?" I asked, and she grimaced.

"I get uncomfortable when you compliment me," she admitted, and I realized that she was cracking the door to her heart open and letting me peek inside.

"Why's that?"

She shook her head, like she was having some sort of internal battle. "Because I don't know what you want, Crew. Like what you really want."

"I want you. I've been telling you that."

"Yeah, but every guy says that."

"I mean it though. I'm not going to disappear when our contract ends. Hell, I'd only chase you even harder to get you to give me a chance."

I watched as her eyes oscillated between looking at me through the screen and somewhere far off in the distance. She wanted to believe me, to trust what I was saying … but she didn't.

"I know Seline talked to you," she said, and I sucked in a long breath, filling my chest and lungs with air.

She figured that I'd somehow gotten insider knowledge that I could use to my advantage. And in a way, I guessed I had but not like Summer was assuming.

"She did. Are you upset?"

"I was."

"She didn't tell me anything that you hadn't hinted to already. Eventually, I would have put the pieces together on my own," I said, and she stared at me, so I continued, "I can't imagine the lines of shit you've heard in the past. It makes me fucking insane to even think about, so I try not to."

"You try not to think about what other guys said to me?" She interrupted my train of thought.

"I can't even think about another man touching you without wanting to break his fucking hand, so yeah. But that's not the point."

"Oh. What is the point then?"

I sat up in the bed, grabbing the extra pillows and stuffing them behind my back. I felt myself getting a little too amped up. "The point is, I can't imagine what you've heard. What lies you've been told. But that's not me. I don't play games. And I'm always upfront and honest with any woman that I'm with," I said and watched as she noticeably winced at my mention of other females.

She wanted me just as much as I wanted her. And we were both possessive of the other. I liked that.

"If I just want to have sex, they're very aware. I don't lie. I don't trick. I don't say cheesy one-liners to get them into bed. I don't have to do any of that."

Summer cleared her throat. "Well, good for you. I'm so happy that all of your past conquests have been so agreeable."

I was fucking this all up. I wasn't even sure how I'd steered us toward the topic of me and other women, but here we were. "I just meant that I want to be with you. I want to date you. I want you by my side at every event and every party. I want to look up in the stands during my games and see your gorgeous face there, cheering me on. I want to come home at night and see you waiting for me in our bed, with our dog."

She sniffed, and it stopped me mid-speech. "How can you be so sure? I'm not trying to be cynical. I'm sincerely asking."

"I don't have the answer to that question. At least, not with words. All I know is how I feel and that I've never been able to picture anyone by my side—until I met you. I always figured I'd be alone. You know?"

Summer stayed silent on the other end as we both watched each other, our eyes never breaking contact. A moment beyond words was brewing between us, that connection deepening. She had to know I was telling the truth.

"When I get back into town, I'm taking you out," I informed her. I would not be taking no for an answer.

She nodded as she said, "Okay," softly into the line.

"And as far as I'm concerned, you're already mine," I said with a grin. "Talk to you tomorrow." I ended the call.

Dropping a bomb like that on Summer and leaving her to contemplate it on her own, where she couldn't argue back defensively, was a little abrupt but hopefully an effective strategy.

Either that or it was going to backfire in my face.

SO F'N EGOTISTICAL

SUMMER

*U*GHHHHHH!!!

Crew was so damn irritating. His ego knew no bounds. Up until the end, that had been the sweetest phone call I'd ever had in my entire life. No man had ever said those kinds of things to me—and meant them. And I sensed that Crew did. That the things he was telling me weren't going to fade with time or once our job ended.

But then he had to go and say that I belonged to him before hanging up on me.

I'm his.

Give. Me. A. Break.

I wasn't his. I wasn't anyone's. And if that was the truth, then why the hell was I so turned on by his demanding mouth?

Something about Crew claiming me was sexy as sin even if it was a tad bit annoying. Crew was turning me into someone I didn't recognize. A woman who hadn't ever ventured this far with a client. A woman who actually liked having a bossy, alpha male in her life.

A girl who enjoyed being told what to do?

Who knew? Not me—that was for damn sure. I thought about calling Seline and getting her opinion but assumed that she'd tell me to get *over* myself and give *in* to Crew. Instead of overthinking, I grabbed the remote, turned on Netflix, and surfed for a new series to lose myself in.

I must have fallen asleep at some point because the sun was streaming through my curtains and Bart's wet nose was nudging my arm.

"You need to go out?" I asked, my voice groggy, and he started wagging his tail, making the bed bounce.

Dragging myself out of the warmth of my covers, I let Bart into my backyard before filling his bowl with food and turning on my coffeemaker. Bart was so funny to watch; his tail wagged like a helicopter blade, in a circle, the entire time that he ate. I was convinced that no one on this earth was happier than Bart was.

Grabbing a cup of coffee, I realized that I'd left my cell phone in my bedroom, and I padded back there to grab it. There were numerous text messages and email alerts and a missed call from Seline. I hadn't even heard my phone ring as I pressed her face to return the call.

"Are you okay?" she asked as she answered.

"Why wouldn't I be okay?"

She made a sound, and I knew instantly that something was wrong. "You haven't seen the headlines today?"

"I just grabbed my phone. What am I missing?"

Has something happened to Crew? Has there been an accident on the field?

"Check your dailies, and I'll hold," she insisted, and that was when I knew it had to be bad.

Scrolling through my inbox and the media alerts I had set up for Crew, I saw a picture of him with an extremely good-looking brunette on his lap from the night before. Her arm was wrapped around him, and they looked … cozy. Zooming in on the picture, I tried to steady my breathing as I read the caption.

LA's new football god making himself at home on and

off the field.

"Hello?!" Seline shouted, redirecting my attention.

"I'm here," I said, barely able to get the words out.

"Are you okay?"

My head spun. Nothing made sense. "Yeah." I inhaled a deep breath and regained my composure. "He called me last night, so he couldn't have been with her."

Instead of arguing with me or telling me I was right, Seline simply said, "I can stop by."

And I knew she would, but there was no point.

"No. I'm good," I lied. I wanted it to be the truth, but my heart was racing, my stomach twisting, and my brain tried to make sense of it all.

"Why do I feel like you're the one being rational right now and I'm the one who wants to kill the guy?"

"Because I know as well as anyone that things aren't always what they seem," I explained, trying like hell to believe my own words.

"Even if …" she rattled off something in French that I didn't understand before switching back to English. "No woman should be touching him like that if he likes you as much as he claims to."

Nodding my head, I made an annoyed huff. "Now, that's something I can agree with."

"Let me know what happens. I gotta go," she said before ending the call.

I took a screenshot of the article, picture included, and texted it to Crew.

Whenever I signed on a new athlete, I set up alerts with their name in it for the duration of our contract. It helped me stay up to date on any potential drama or if where we were looking to live got leaked, et cetera. The more information I had on my client, the better I could be at my job.

My phone rang immediately. I answered but didn't say a word.

"That is not at all what it looks like," Crew said, breathing hard into the phone like he'd been working out or something.

"Tell me what it was then."

"I told you that I was going out with the guys' last night, remember?"

"Yes."

"A bunch of chicks eventually showed up. They must

have found out we were there. That one in particular asked for a photo, and when I said yes, she sat on my lap and wrapped herself around me like a snake," he explained, and I believed him. "The second the picture was taken, I got her off me."

"Good," I said without thinking.

"You're jealous?" He was genuinely asking and wasn't at all being cocky about it.

"Yes," I admitted because I was. I hated seeing some gorgeous female draped all over him like he was her property.

"It will never happen again," he said.

"I really didn't like waking up to that."

"It won't happen again, Duchess. I promise." He reinforced another time. "No woman touches me who isn't you."

"Damn straight," I breathed out, and he laughed.

"My woman is feisty."

"Apparently," I said because my feelings about this were even shocking to me.

"Summer"—Crew's tone turned even more serious— "I'm yours already too. Just so we're clear."

Damn.

How could I ever stay mad at this man when he kept saying things like that?

HE'S HOME

SUMMER

THE LAST FEW days had felt like they took a million years. Seline had been blowing me off, claiming that work was running her ragged, so I'd been alone with my thoughts.

Bart and I were currently sitting in my car, waiting for Crew to exit the airport. He'd already sent me a text that he landed, had his luggage, and was coming out. I was nervous.

My whole insides felt like wild animals were running rampant, trampling everything in sight. Bart saw him before I did, his tail wagging as he started whining.

"See your dad?" I asked as I noticed Crew's frame heading straight toward us.

He pulled open the rear seat, petted Bart, and tossed

his luggage inside before getting into the passenger seat and leaning toward me. My entire body shivered with that look, and before I knew it, his hand was snaking around the back of my neck as he pulled me toward him, his lips meeting mine without warning. My mouth opened to him easily as his tongue found its way inside, like we'd done this a million times before. He tasted like spearmint mixed with heat, and I never wanted him to stop. Crew's lips were soft and all-consuming.

When he broke the kiss, my eyes refused to open, and my body refused to move.

"Hey, Duchess," he said, forcing my eyes to finally give in and open. Crew sat there, looking smug as he ran a finger across his bottom lip. "I missed you."

"Uh-huh," was all I managed to say before he was leaning back over, kissing me again.

His tongue had a mind of its own, claiming my mouth, forcing me to moan out in response against him.

"Let's take this somewhere more private," he said, and I hit the gas without hesitation.

Crew's hand snaked across the center console before finding my thigh and resting there, his thumb moving back and forth across my bare skin. It was like once I'd given him the green light to touch me, he couldn't stop. Not that I was complaining. I liked the way his hand felt there.

"So, the rest of the trip was good? The guys still love you?" I gave him a quick look to find that he was staring at me. "Stop staring," I said, embarrassed.

"Not a chance," he countered. "And, yeah, it was really good. We're going to have a fun season."

"Fun, huh?" I teased.

"Yep. Fun because we're going to win."

That made me laugh out loud. Every pro athlete claimed they were going to win. They weren't quitters.

"Of course you are."

"How was Bart while I was gone?" he asked me but turned his body away to give his dog some attention.

Bart licked his cheek, his tail hitting the side of my car as he wagged it. When Crew's hand left my leg, I almost grabbed it and put it back but stopped myself from going that far.

"He's such a good boy. Like the perfect dog, honestly."

"It's his demeanor. He's always been that way. Low

maintenance and happy." Crew laughed as he kissed Bart's nose.

I realized that I was going to miss having Bart around. I loved our evening and afternoon walks, spending time together on the beach and how everyone loved him.

"You're making that face again," Crew announced, and I frowned to cover whatever I was doing. "The one where you're overthinking."

"I was just thinking about Bart and how we'd gotten into a routine. And how I was going to be bored without him."

Crew's hand was back on my leg, squeezing and kneading. "I'll share him with you. Plus, we're going to have to figure out what to do when I'm on the road."

I moved the lever up to activate my turn signal as I navigated off of the freeway and onto the side streets toward Crew's rental home. "What do you mean, when you're on the road?"

"Well, if you're with me at my away games, what are we going to do with Bart? Can he come too? That would mean you'd have to drive, and we'd have to find a hotel that took dogs. But if you don't come to every away game, then you and Bart can hang together until I get back."

I looked at him like he was a madman, and then I stared back at the road, my head shaking back and forth. "Have you planned out our whole life without talking to me about it?"

"I've been thinking about the details a bit, yeah."

"I can see that," I said as I stopped outside of his gate, rolled down my window, and punched the code in. The iron gates swung open, and I pulled inside, making sure it closed behind us.

Crew's hand stopped me. "Don't get upset. I wasn't trying to be controlling. I really was just thinking about all of our options, and I don't know." He looked actually nervous. "I really don't want to fuck this up."

"Then, don't," I said before opening the driver's door and hopping out.

Reaching for the back door, I pulled it open before Crew could get to his, and Bart happily jumped down and ran into the grass, rolling on his back like he'd never been happier.

I watched as Crew grabbed his bag and hauled it over his shoulder before looking at me.

"Come inside?" It was a question instead of a demand, but I'd already planned on coming in.

I figured we had some business to discuss anyway, if nothing else, but the second we walked through the front door, the smell of food hit me.

"How? Is someone in here?" I looked back over my shoulder. I hadn't noticed any other cars in the driveway or parked in front of his house.

Crew dropped his duffel to the floor and reached for my hand. "I had some help," he said as he pulled me toward the kitchen, where the table was set for two with a vase of fresh flowers and two unlit candles. He grabbed the lighter that was sitting between them, flicked it to life, and lit them before walking toward his stove, where pots and pans sat with lids on.

"How did you coordinate this?" I grinned, impressed that he'd done something so romantic without any help from me.

"Hey," he started to complain. "I'm a resourceful guy. I can figure things out." When I didn't say anything in response but narrowed my eyes and put my hands on my hips, he blew out a breath and said, "Seline."

I started laughing. I should have known. "You two are something else."

"It was all my idea, but I needed a little help. And who knows you better than your best friend?"

"That's why she's been avoiding my calls the last two days. She can't keep a secret from me if her life depended on it," I said before it hit me. "But wait, I can't believe you got her to help you after the photos that were published."

Crew shifted on his feet. "Oh. She hung up on me twice. By the third call, I had to wait while she yelled at me in French for, like, ten minutes before switching to English."

"Sounds about right."

"We're good now though. At least, I think we are." He glanced down at the food before giving me a look. "She wouldn't poison you, right?"

"She likes my business too much," I said with a chuckle.

Before I knew it, Crew was back on me, his hands wrapped around my waist as he pulled me against him. "I want to eat this food, but I want to eat you first."

"You have such a dirty mouth," I pretended to

complain, but I was turned on, and we both knew it. Instead of pulling away from him, my hips moved into his, and I started grinding.

He leaned down, lifted my body in his arms as Bart barked, and started walking down the hall, staring at me the entire time. "I want you, Summer. I can't wait another fucking second to be inside you. Please don't ask me to."

I licked my lips. "I'm not."

"Thank God," he said as he deposited me on top of the bed in his massive room and went to work on untying my shoes and removing my socks before working his way up my long legs and toward my jean shorts. His hands were on the button and then the zipper, and before I knew it, I was bare from the waist down. He'd not only pulled off my shorts, but my thong as well.

"I've wanted this since the first time I saw you," he said before grabbing my legs and yanking my body down. "Come here, Summer."

I wasn't sure exactly what he wanted, but I moved off of the bed anyway. He turned me around, so my ass was in his face as he placed his hand on my lower back and pushed.

"Bend over," he demanded, and I did as he'd asked.

He buried his face in me. His tongue licking my ass, his fingers spreading me open. I'd never felt so vulnerable before, but Crew made me feel sexy, desired, and delicious. He moaned as he ate my ass before he moved his tongue toward my pussy, keeping his thumb pressed against my other hole, not quite moving all the way in. Just the pressure of him pushing there was almost enough to send me over the edge.

His hands were back on my waist as he flipped me around, so I was on my back. My legs wrapped around his shoulders as he continued eating my pussy and playing with my ass.

"I knew you'd taste this good. I fucking dreamed about it," he said, his tongue hitting my clit over and over again.

I reached for his head, and my nails dug into his scalp, my legs tightening on his shoulders as my orgasm built. "Crew, I'm going to come."

His finger pushed inside my other hole as he continued to eat my pussy at the same time, and the feeling was so overwhelming that I came instantly, his name a song on my lips as I repeated it over and over and over again.

"Jesus," he breathed out, his face wet with me as he wiped at it with the back of his hand.

I wanted to return the favor. I planned on putting him in my mouth, but he peeled off the rest of my clothes before telling me not to move an inch.

So demanding.

I watched as he undressed, noting the way his muscles flexed, his abs contracting as he breathed, and when his dick sprang free from his boxer briefs, I swore my eyes almost bulged out of my head at the glorious sight. That was a cock from the gods.

"I want you every way at once," he said as his body hovered over mine.

The tip of his dick was at my entrance, and I wiggled my hips to make him go in, but he grinned and shook his head, reminding me that I was not even remotely in control.

In one movement, he pushed himself inside of me, and I made an uncomfortable sound in response before my body adjusted to him.

"Summer ..." Crew's voice strained, his eyes closing and opening before he started kissing me. He moved slow as he fucked me, and his kisses moved even slower.

"You feel so good," I said, hoping he knew that I was enjoying this as much as he was.

He refused to stop kissing me. His lips attached to mine as his tongue darted in and out. I was lost in the way kissing him felt, the way his dick felt inside of me, and the feeling of his skin on mine. There were so many senses in play; I wasn't sure which one to focus on.

When he reached for my body with both hands, I knew we were about to switch positions, but I wasn't sure to what exactly. He tried to move onto his back, so I could get on top without having us come unattached, but it was impossible. He slipped out, and I straddled his body, grabbing his cock with one hand as I lowered myself on top of it and dropped all the way down.

"You feel like you're stabbing me in the ribs," I said, expecting him to laugh, but his expression was serious and focused.

"I want you to fuck me, Summer," he said the words like I was going to get to control the pace, but when his hands gripped my hip bones and started bouncing me up and down on him, I knew that he was still calling the shots.

He moved me quicker, faster, my body rising up on his slickness before slamming back down again. All at his pace. His hips bucked up into me, the sound of our bodies slapping against each other, echoing in the room as sweat started forming at the base of my neck.

"Kiss me," Crew said, his green eyes staring deep into mine.

I leaned down to kiss him, my hips still grinding up and down on him like a pogo stick as we kissed and fucked like we had been made for one another.

"I'm going to come so fucking hard," Crew breathed out as our bodies moved even faster than they had been.

I felt him growing even bigger inside me even though that felt damn near impossible.

"Yes, Crew, fuck me. Fuck me," I exclaimed as his body started convulsing and pulsing inside me.

He reached for my neck and pulled me back down to kiss him again.

"That was incredible," he said between kisses.

"Yeah, it was," I agreed.

THAT'S HOW YOU KILL A MAN

CREW

*J*ESUS *H. CHRIST.*

Fucking like that was how a man went to die. Or how he wanted to die. On the altar of his woman, his dick still hard inside her while she yelled his name like it was the only thing in the world that mattered.

Take your last breath, boys. This is how we're going out.

I was a proper gentleman after sex and fed Summer until she couldn't eat another bite. The chef Seline had gotten for me was exquisite. A third-generation Italian who had only been in the States a few years. He had started a restaurant locally and flew in fresh ingredients direct from Italy. It tasted unlike anything I'd ever eaten; the pasta was so ... *light.*

And even though I didn't want her to go back to her own house, I begrudgingly agreed to let her but not without some pouting first. We were talking lips stuck out, puppy-dog eyes, and some actual groveling.

It didn't work.

"Thank you for tonight," she said, a smile on her face as I tucked some loose strands behind her ear and kissed the nape of her neck. She pulled away with a giggle. "I know what you're trying to do," she accused, and I faked innocent.

"What? A guy can't kiss his girlfriend good night?" I said, and her eyes widened for a split second before she recovered. I reached for her chin and tilted her face upward. "Summer, I told you, I'm already yours. If you think that I can walk away from you now, you're severely mistaken."

She faked a cough, her fist punching her chest. "Crew."

"Say it," I demanded.

"Say what?"

"Say I'm your *boyfriend*." I dragged the word out, acting like a freaking preschooler.

Her lips twisted up into a smile that she tried to force into a frown but failed. "Fine. You are. I guess."

Grabbing her waist, I pulled her up against me, my dick hard again. "That's not what I asked. And it didn't sound very convincing. Is it so bad, being my girlfriend?" I asked, kissing random parts of her as I teased her.

"That was too many questions. I forgot them all," she breathed out, sounding exasperated and turned on.

Her hips started to push into my body, and if I didn't stop this now, I'd fuck her right here on the grass without a care in the world.

"Who am I?"

"Crew Maxwell."

"Your?"

"My?"

"Your what?" I pushed.

"My quarterback," she answered.

"Summer," I growled, taking her bottom lip in my mouth and biting it until she whimpered.

"My boyfriend. You're my boyfriend," she agreed, not sounding the least bit convinced. I wasn't sure if it was because she didn't believe me or if she hadn't had an actual boyfriend in so long that the term was strange at this point.

"Yes, I am." I moved my tongue into her mouth and reminded her who she belonged to. She was mine. I was hers. And there wasn't a moment where I saw that fact changing. "And I'll see you tomorrow."

"You will? I mean, of course you will. We still have work to do."

"Yes, I will," I reassured her. "And not because of work."

Even though she wasn't necessarily acting like it, I knew some part of her had to be worried that since she'd given in to me, I'd disappear. But I wasn't going anywhere.

Especially not after tonight.

Why on earth would I ever willingly walk away from a woman like her

I opened the car door for her and helped her inside before giving her another kiss. "Call me when you get home, so I know you're safe."

Her jaw dropped slightly before she slammed it shut and pursed her lips together.

"What? Did I say something wrong?"

"No." She shook her head. "That's a guy test that no guys pass anymore."

I replayed her words one more time before giving up. "It's a what that what?" I asked, stumbling over my own thoughts.

"Nothing." She waved me off. "I'll call you," she said as she started the engine.

As soon as she cleared my driveway and the gate closed, I turned to walk back inside and clean the dinner dishes. I really didn't want to, and I was tempted to leave them until the next morning, but I knew I wouldn't want to deal with them then either. It was now or never.

I filled half of the sink with hot water and soap when my phone rang. I looked down at it, wondering who it could be when I saw Summer's name. Wiping my hand on a dish towel, I pressed Accept to answer the call.

"Summer? Is everything okay?" I got worried that she'd gotten into an accident or something.

"I'm fine," she said, and I realized how quiet it was in the background.

"You're not home already, are you?"

She laughed. "Yep."

"You literally just left my place."

"I know."

"Wait. Summer, how far away do you live?"

She started laughing again into the phone line. "Not far."

"How far is not far?"

"Pretty close."

"Summer, where the hell are you?"

"Three blocks away," she answered. "Happy?"

"You live three blocks away from me, and you're not here right now?"

"Yes."

"You're lucky I don't hook Bart up to his leash and have him lead the way. I'm sure he knows it," I threatened as Bart started wagging his tail and jumping up and down.

"He'd take you to the beach and plop his happy ass right down in the middle of the sand," she said, and I knew she was probably right. "Are you mad?"

"No. Of course not." I wasn't … *mad.* "Just a little surprised, is all."

"I know. Sorry. I wasn't going to tell you at all, but

now that you're my—" She stopped short of saying the word out loud again, and I filled it in for her.

"Boyfriend. Now that I'm your boyfriend."

"Yeah. That. I guess you need to know these things."

"Good night, Summer. See you tomorrow."

"Night," she said, her tone sounding actually surprised that I was letting her off the hook so easily.

But her man had a shitload of dishes that apparently weren't going to wash themselves.

WE EASILY FELL into a routine over the next couple of weeks. I found myself learning to navigate the LA traffic and freeways, and even though both sucked, it wasn't like I could control them. Some days, it took me forty minutes to get back home, and others, it took me almost two hours. But it was all worth it. I loved living in Manhattan Beach.

Somehow, in the midst of it all, I'd convinced this amazing woman to be at my place, waiting for me when I got home from practice every day. There was nothing that I loved more than walking through the front door and seeing her there with Bart. It filled me with a sort of peace and stability that I'd never had before. I always wondered what kind of woman would make me give up my single life, and I knew without a shadow of a doubt that it couldn't have been any other woman. It had to be her.

Which was why we were currently house-hunting from a secret file folder that Seline had given Summer while I was away with the team. None of the homes had hit the market yet but were still forthcoming. I was getting to see them early, thanks to both Seline and my occupation.

"What do you think?" I asked against Summer's neck as I held her hand tightly in mine.

"It's beautiful. But a little over the top, don't you think?" She looked at me and shrugged. "I'm just saying, do you really need eight bathrooms?"

"You're right. You're totally right." I shook my head because it was easy to get lost in a stunning home when you could technically afford it but didn't really need it.

"Okay, you two." Seline stepped between us, breaking our contact, and I practically attacked her. "I have one last stop. It's not on any list, but I know you're going to love it."

"Wait, what is it? One I don't even know about?"

Summer asked her best friend, looking annoyed.

"It's new construction. Still being built, but it's almost done," she said, and Summer nodded like that made complete and total sense to her.

"Let's see it," I said before heading to my G-Wagon. Now that Summer and I were a couple, I insisted on driving us everywhere. It was my job to take care of my woman, and part of that, in my opinion, was driving.

"Any idea where we're headed?" I asked Summer once we were in my car.

"No. I don't even know of any new construction within the city limits. Unless it was a teardown."

"Meaning?"

"It's exactly what it sounds like. They tear down the old house and build a brand-new one on the existing land. It actually happens a lot out here."

"And the new house is better than the old one?"

Summer laughed. "Oh, yeah. I mean, they really know how to make use of a limited amount of space these days. So, instead of building larger homes that they don't have room for, they build up."

"Gotcha," I said as I followed Seline's black Mercedes

around the tiny streets.

When her brake lights lit up and she pulled to a stop in front of what looked like a three-story gray-and-white home, I pulled in behind her and did the same as I eyed the house, still lined with construction cones and workers finishing up the job.

Seline was at my door in a flash. "Come on."

I popped open my door before asking, "We can go in?"

"It's practically done. Just finishing up the backyard and some other details that were weather-related pushbacks."

I reached for Summer's hand again, threading my fingers through hers as we walked toward the three-car garage and the front door.

"It's three stories with a rooftop view of the ocean," Seline said as my eyes grew wide.

Even Summer looked impressed as we stepped inside. The details were immaculate. Dark blue paint with slate-gray tiles greeted us. There was a massive beechwood table with black iron candleholders lining the walls. It was fucking stunning. And masculine.

"I love this," I breathed out, and Summer looked at me,

practically foaming at the mouth.

"It's unbelievably appealing," she agreed, and we took in the rest of the four-bedroom, four-and-a-half-bath home. There wasn't a single detail that I would change. It was like they'd built this home with me in mind.

"You have to see the best part." Seline waved us toward the hidden staircase.

"Holy shit," Summer squealed once we reached the top. "I'm never leaving."

The dark-blue and slate-gray color pattern continued throughout the covered rooftop deck. Half of the railing was lined with wood for privacy while the other half had some sort of smoked glass that you could see everything through. The ocean was visible from every angle. There were couches, multiple tables, hanging lanterns, a full-size fireplace, and a mounted TV.

Walking to the edge, I glanced down to see the small backyard. Summer had been right when she mentioned the plots of land here not being very large, but what they'd managed to build on it was pretty close to perfect. The yard might not be huge, but it was still plenty big for Bart. Not to mention, privacy gates and walls lined the home. People might know that I lived here, but they wouldn't be able to get in or gain access. At least, not without some serious effort.

Seline settled in next to me and asked, "What do you think?"

I paused before glancing at Summer, who was making herself at home on one of the couches.

"Can we keep it?" Summer asked as soon as our eyes met across the open space.

"Think she means it?" I wondered out loud, and Seline clapped her hands together as Summer hopped up from the couch and joined us at the balcony.

"Is this the one? This is the one, right?"

"Do you like it?"

"I love it," she exclaimed.

"Would you live here?"

"I might never leave here," she answered with a giggle, and I looked at Seline.

"I think we'll take it," I said, and the girls started hugging before Seline grew serious.

"Okay. I have work to do. Take my girl somewhere to celebrate," Seline insisted.

"You mean, *my* girl," I countered, and she pretended not to hear me.

WHEN CONTRACTS END

SUMMER

CREW HAD BOUGHT the house that dreams were made of and was set to move in, in approximately thirteen days, which also signaled the official end of our contract. It was perfect timing because we'd get him all settled before the season officially started, and it would be one less thing for him to worry about while he was playing for a new team, in a new city.

I didn't even have another client lined up yet. My schedule had always been pretty packed with very few open days, but here I was, leaving myself available to travel with Crew if he wanted me to.

So, why was the thought suddenly so terrifying? Why was I afraid that we were about to end?

"You okay?" he asked as we snuggled on the couch in

his rental house, Bart sitting next to me instead of his true owner.

"Yeah. Just thinking about the end of our contract," I said with a wince.

"Why?" He turned his body to face mine as he waited for me to respond to his question.

I hated sounding insecure, so I wasn't sure what to say that would help me come off as less needy, so I said nothing and stared into his green eyes instead.

"Summer, we're not ending because our contract is."

"I know," I said, followed by an uncomfortable laugh. Clearly, I didn't know.

"Do you? I bought us a house," he explained, and I reared back at the use of the word *us*.

"You bought yourself a house." I wasn't purposefully trying to be difficult, just realistic.

My name wasn't on the title. It wasn't my house. It was his. He was paying for it, not me. I hadn't contributed a single dime toward it, and I hadn't planned on it either.

"I bought a house that *you* loved," he emphasized. "A home you said you never wanted to leave."

"Oh," was all I could formulate as his words hit me.

He bought the house because I love it?

"I want you to move in with me."

I cleared my throat. "You want me to what?"

"I was going to play it cool and wait until you started spending the night every night and then tell you that you already lived with me anyway, so you should just bring your things over," he said, like his words were no big deal at all when they were absolutely life-changing.

"Crew." I shook my head. I was not an irrational woman. I didn't jump into things with both feet and question them later.

"I know what you're going to say," he started, and I cocked my head to the side and gave him a smirk.

"What am I going to say?" I folded my arms across my chest and waited.

"That it's too fast. We should take our time. Make sure it's right, blah, blah," he said, and I bit back the laugh bubbling in my throat because he was right. "Am I wrong?"

"No," I responded, annoyed that he knew me so well.

He pushed up from the couch and walked toward the window, staring out of it. I followed him, wrapping my arms around his middle and leaning my head against his back.

"Don't be upset with me."

Crew turned around, keeping my arms in place with his as he faced me. "I'm not. I know that not rushing is the right thing to do, but I just ..." He maneuvered out of my grip and ran his hands across his face as he started walking away.

"What? What's the matter?" I felt so lost, so unsure of what was going on in his head.

We'd just started dating. And, yes, it had been incredible and unbelievably easy so far, but we hadn't even gotten into the start of the football season yet. There was still so much to experience and go through as a couple.

What if we weren't any good at it? What if it was too hard for me? What if the other women were something I didn't want to deal with on a daily basis?

I had a lot of questions and concerns. Things I'd never voiced to Crew yet. Keeping them to myself had just seemed like the better option up until this point.

Crew eventually walked himself into the kitchen, and

he leaned his elbows on top of the granite as he watched me. "I know it's fast. I do. But I also know that you're it for me." He put a hand up to stop me from disagreeing. "You can tell me it's too soon to know. But you'd be wrong. I know." He looked straight at me, his face deadly serious. "I know."

I'd never in my life had someone be so sure about me and say it out loud and to my face before. It was a surreal feeling to know that this incredible man thought that he wanted to be with me forever. But there was still that little part of my brain that refused to give in. It refused to be romanced. It absolutely would not swoon.

"I have a compromise," I said as I headed toward him. When I reached the kitchen, I pulled out a barstool and sat down across from him.

"I'm listening."

"My lease is up in a few months."

Even though I had plenty of money saved and actually owned two homes in other states, I was currently renting the house I lived in. Seline had found it for me at an absolute steal years ago. It had been in the same family for generations and was all paid off, so they charged me next to nothing to live there and keep it up. I knew that they would let me continue to stay for as long as I wanted and that moving would probably be a surprise to them, but maybe it was time.

Crew's face actually lit up as he looked at me. "It is?"

"Mmhmm."

"So, what you're saying is that if things are still good with us, which they will be, you'll move in with me and Bart?" He headed around the granite counter, running his fingers across the top as he made his way toward me.

"I don't see why not," I said even though my heart was pounding and my head was screaming with fear.

"I'm going to make you so fucking happy." Crew was standing in between my legs now, his large hands cupping my face as he leaned down to kiss me.

It wasn't sweet or gentle. It was a kiss without time. It had nothing to do with how long we'd known each other or how long we'd been dating. That kiss was punishing, deep, and hard. It was the kind of kiss that reminded you of exactly who you belonged to, who made your body bend and curve at their whim, who claimed you wherever they damn well pleased, without regard for anyone else.

Crew picked me up and placed my body on top of the cold granite, and I squirmed as he pulled my shorts down and started feasting on my already-wet pussy, telling me that he'd never get tired of tasting me. Once he finished making me orgasm, using his tongue and fingers in a way I'd never understand, he climbed on top of the table and thrust himself inside of me without warning or ease. His large cock still made me gasp on entry, but my body quickly adjusted to his size, craving more.

"I want to break this fucking counter," he breathed out against me, his hips moving fast and deep.

"I don't care what you do as long as you don't stop," I said, looking deep into his eyes. I reached for his ass, my fingers digging in as I silently pleaded for him to fuck me harder, deeper, and faster.

Sex had never been like this before. I'd never been so unquenched, so utterly hungry for more all. The. Time. When he released inside of me, his body falling on top of mine, sweaty and breathing hard, I realized that I was falling in love with this man. And I wanted a future with him.

He'd better not mess it up.

JOINT ACCOUNT

SUMMER

OUR CONTRACT HAD officially ended the day we moved Crew into the house. Crew had refused to decorate without me and insisted that I bring over some of my favorite things so that it would feel more like "ours" whenever I came over.

Which was all the time, just like he always said it would be. I rarely spent the night at my own place anymore, hating being away from him and Bart. And the house really did feel like our home. Well, as much as it could when I wasn't contributing financially to it.

It was weird, having my boyfriend continue to pay me, and I almost stopped taking his direct deposits, but he wouldn't hear of it, threatening to buy me something so extreme that I'd be embarrassed but unable to refuse it. So,

I opened a joint account with the money instead. When I told him what I had done and handed him his own debit card, I swore he almost teared up.

"No one has ever taken care of me before, Summer," he said as he sniffed and turned away from me, clearly not wanting me to witness him getting choked up.

"Well, get used to it," I said even though I knew the feeling all too well. It was uncomfortable as hell.

"This is why you always push back on me," he said, as if some level of understanding had only just now dawned on him.

"It's not entirely comfortable to have someone do things for you when you're used to doing them by yourself."

"I don't think anyone's ever wanted to do things for me before. No one's ever even tried," he said, and I felt sad for him.

Sure, I wasn't a relationship expert by any means, but I'd never thought about being Crew from Crew's point of view.

He went on to explain that he'd never trusted anyone before meeting me. He'd dated plenty of women, but he'd

145

mostly felt used. He knew they didn't want the man off the football field. They wanted the famous football player, the money, and the publicity. I understood the sentiment of feeling used. Maybe that was why we worked so well together. I wasn't a user and didn't need his status.

"You and I are both used to being independent. We're going to have to learn how to receive from one another," I explained, and he blew out a breath.

"I'll think about it," he said with a grimace before disappearing back down the stairs.

THE NEXT TIME I checked our joint account balance, my eyes practically bugged out of my head. Crew had deposited ten thousand dollars into it.

"Crew!" I shouted from the rooftop balcony, hoping he could hear me from below.

"What's up, Duchess?" he shouted back.

"Why is there an extra ten grand in our joint account?" I screamed before realizing that maybe I shouldn't be shouting about this topic where everyone could overhear and tell TMZ or some other gossip site. "Can you come up here, please?"

He appeared in front of me in a flash. "It's not a joint account if only you put money in it," he explained, and I bit back a smile.

"That's ridiculous."

"Me? You started it!" he complained, and I couldn't really argue because I had opened the account with a hefty sum.

"Well, now, we have so much money in there that the bank is going to start calling me."

They did that sometimes. Once you reached a certain balance, they wanted you to open a different kind of account or start investing with one of their people.

"I figured that it could be our vacation account." Crew shrugged.

"Vacation account?" I asked because we hadn't really talked about what we were going to do with the account, only that we'd opened it.

"Yeah. We'll put money in there that we'll only use for travel and trips."

I pondered what he was saying for all of two seconds before nodding my head like crazy. "That's a great idea! I love it!"

Crew looked relieved, but I was completely convinced and overly excited.

"Vacation account for the win!" I shouted, thrusting a fist into the air.

"For the win!" he repeated with a laugh.

THE SEASON STARTED with a bang. Crew and his team were unstoppable and currently undefeated. But it was still early, and there was a lot of football left to play.

I'd met a couple of the girlfriends, but I hadn't really bonded with any yet. We weren't always seated in the same sections, so getting to know them made it difficult. I hoped that changed as the season went on and we spent more time together, maybe on road games.

The wives were a different breed altogether. They seemed to separate themselves from the rest of us, acting like they were on a level we might not ever get to. Which was honestly fair, if you thought about it. Girlfriends could come and go. Wives assumed they were forever.

As I headed toward the underground tunnel, my pass

firmly in place around my neck, nothing mattered, except seeing my man. Watching him on the field was one thing, but seeing his face when he walked through the locker room door was something else entirely.

"Never thought I'd see the day when one of my guys tied you down, Summer." Coach Huxley suddenly appeared at my side.

I hadn't expected to see him there. At least he was in a good mood since the team had just won; otherwise, I might have done my best to run and hide.

"You and me both," I agreed with a smile.

"I know they've all tried."

"That they have, Coach."

He laughed. "Well, if he hurts you, let me know. I'll bench his ass."

"Really?" I questioned because even though I knew that Coach Huxley loved me and the job I did for him, I didn't think he'd do something that petty for someone like me.

"Hell no, not really. Unless he's losing. Then, I will. And I'll say it's because he hurt you."

"Fair enough," I answered with a laugh as Coach

continued walking down the semi-darkened tunnel toward some office in the back.

"There's my woman." Crew's voice echoed into the hallway as he stepped out of the locker room doors before anyone else, the sound of them slamming shut behind him making a little kid jump.

Pulling me into his arms, Crew lifted me in the air and kissed me for all the other girlfriends and wives to see before putting me down gently and wrapping a strong arm around me. "I missed you," he said against my cheek, his hair still wet from his shower.

I actually lived for this. The way Crew claimed me, made sure everyone knew I was his, and never gave the impression to any other woman that he was available. It was the constant reassurance that I secretly needed. And Crew gave it without me ever having to ask. I could tell the other women were jealous or envious of the affection Crew always showed, and I couldn't even blame them. I'd feel the same way if it wasn't happening to me.

"Where's Seline?" Crew asked as he held my hand and pulled me toward the exit.

"She had to leave. She has a date." I wiggled my

eyebrows at him, and he made a face.

"With who? Did you vet him?"

Crew was very defensive over the people he cared about, and that now included my best friend.

"Seline's a big girl, and she can take care of herself," I said, knowing that my response would only make him crazy.

We'd lived our whole lives without Crew around or taking care of us, but he refused to accept that logic.

"Summer"—he shook his head slowly—"tell me you're joking."

I bit out a soft laugh. "I have all of his information here." I pointed at my cell phone.

I'd taken a picture of him and forced him to give me all of his pertinent information, like where he was staying out here, his permanent address, and the car he was driving.

You couldn't be too safe these days.

"I swear, you two are trying to kill me," he breathed out. "The guy had better not be some douche like the last one."

"He's not," I reassured him, and he stopped walking to

look me in the eyes.

The last guy Seline had gone out with was a pathological liar. He pretended to be rich, but he was renting all of his things—that included the Rolex watch he wore on his wrist. It was all some elaborate *fake it till you make it* BS that everyone around him, including me at first, had bought into.

"How can you be so sure?"

" 'Cause it's Caleb Crawley," I said, knowing that the name would get a reaction out of him.

He instantly dropped my hand and reared back. "Caleb Crawley? Like my old running back, Caleb Crawley?"

"Yep."

"How?"

"He was here today. Sitting right next to us. So, in essence, it's all your fault."

Caleb was an ex-pro football player who had played with Crew for years. He'd gotten injured last season and realized that he wasn't going to make a comeback the way he wanted, so he medically retired.

"Why was he here? What's he doing in LA?"

"Apparently interviewing for a job," I said because I

hadn't gotten all of those details exactly.

And it also didn't feel like my story to tell. If Caleb ended up getting the job, he'd be working directly with Crew, and he should be the one to tell him, not me.

Crew stayed quiet for a minute before we started walking again. "I approve of this," he said, like his opinion was the only thing that mattered.

"I'm sure Seline will be relieved to hear it," I said in my most smart-ass tone of voice.

Nothing and no one was going to tell Seline who to date, not even Crew. Not even when he was right.

"Where are they? Let's go crash their date." He was dead serious. "I know you know where they are, Summer. Come on. Give me this," he begged, and I tried to be strong, knowing that I was going to cave and give in to his demands. It sounded like too much fun anyway.

"Fine. But I'm driving."

"The G-wagon?" His voice broke as he asked the question, and I held my hand out, waiting for him to hand over the keys.

I'd taken a car here, per usual. It made no sense for both of us to drive to the stadium when we always ended up leaving together and at the same time.

"Keys or no intel," I threatened, and he reached into his pocket, pulled out the key fob, and dropped it into my hand.

Seline was going to kill me, but I knew she'd get over it.

MY BEST SEASON YET

CREW

W E WERE HEADING into the playoffs, and I knew in my fucking guts that we were going to play in the Super Bowl this year. This had been my best season ever, and Summer had had everything to do with it even though if you asked her, she'd say she didn't do a damn thing. She wasn't on the field, and she didn't catch the ball or throw it or get tackled, according to her. But the truth was that there was something to be said about being sublimely happy on the inside. It spilled over into the rest of your life and everything else that you did, work included. Hell, work especially.

I succeeded without trying. Opportunities literally fell into my lap. I had inked a multimillion-dollar deal with Adidas instead of Nike, which caused all sorts of waves online, but mostly, it had ended up giving me a shit-ton of publicity. I was also set to be the new face of Under Armour, launching in the fall—another controversial topic that had done nothing but expand my reach and audience.

Summer had yet to take on another client, and if I had it my way, she never would again. But I knew that was selfish and wrong of me to hope for. It wasn't that I didn't want her working with athletes anymore; it was just that I wanted her with me all the time. And if she was working for them, she wouldn't be able to travel with me. My life just wasn't the same without her in it.

Which was why when Summer's lease had ended, she'd happily moved in with me, like I'd asked her all those months ago. It had been an easy transition, considering that we were always together anyway, but I wasn't sure what I would have done had she re-signed on her place for another year.

Nothing.

I would have done nothing, but I would have felt shitty inside and wondered why she didn't want to live with me and Bart.

Speaking of, Bart was happier that she lived with us

full-time too. He'd pouted whenever she left, sitting at the front door, waiting for her to walk back through it. It was like he never understood where she had gone off to, and he hated when she was gone. Somewhere along the way, I'd lost my dog, and he'd become hers. I guessed we both were.

"Are you nervous?" Summer's voice interrupted my thoughts, and I turned to look at my gorgeous girlfriend, knowing that she would be my fiancée soon.

"For the game?" I asked, and she grinned.

"Yeah. Are you? Do you get nervous ever?"

"Nah. Not really."

"Seriously?" she asked, running her fingers down the length of my arm, stopping short at the waistband of my workout shorts.

"It's my job. I'm good at my job," I said, grabbing her hand and bringing it up toward my mouth. Moving her fingers apart, I started sucking on one of them, and her head rolled back as she moaned.

"We don't have time for this," she said in a whispered tone but didn't move away.

"They can wait," I growled as I pressed her against the

hotel room wall and did my best not to tear the clothes from her body.

"Be quick," she demanded.

"I'm never quick."

"I know." She looked me in the eyes, her blue ones sparkling in response. "So, fuck me hard and fast for once."

"Damn," I bit back, almost offended. "Do I not fuck you well enough, Duchess?"

She stayed quiet, and I leaned forward, taking her lip between my teeth and biting down a little too hard. She whimpered, her hand reaching toward her mouth, and I noticed the drop of blood there. Before I could apologize, she was leaning forward and biting me back.

I spun her body around, forcing her to face the wall, and I pulled the skirt she was wearing up over her ass and moved her thong to the side. Moving my cock toward her entrance, I plunged as deep as she would take me before doing it all over again. She gasped before taking it like a champ, her hands splayed across the wall, her fingers trying to dig holes into it.

"Yes, Crew, just like that." Her voice was muffled, but

I still heard her requests as I fucked her as hard as I could over and over and over again.

"Damn, Duchess, you feel so fucking tight around me," I said, my breathing already growing labored as her hair spilled down her back and between our bodies.

Before I knew it, she was reaching her hand back and grabbing the base of my dick. She held it, fisting me tightly as I continued.

"Oh damn." I had no idea what she was doing to me, but my dick certainly liked it.

I kept up my pace, and her grip only tightened. I was going to come, and I wasn't even going to be embarrassed about how fast it happened.

When I exploded inside her, filling her with me, she finally let go of my dick and turned around, a grin on her face.

"What was that?" I asked, barely able to get the words out.

"I don't know. I read about it in a book and thought I'd try it. I guess it works."

"It certainly did. But you didn't come," I said, knowing full well that I was the only one truly satisfied. It irked me more than I cared to admit.

"You can make it up to me later," she said as she straightened her skirt.

Little did she know, I planned on it. In more ways than one.

"Come on. They're waiting." She redid her lipstick, making her mouth perfectly lined and colored. I preferred it naked, like the rest of her.

"They can't leave without me," I groaned even though I didn't mean it. It was a dick move to make the other guys on the team wait for you, and I was no prima donna.

We walked out of the room hand in hand, and once we were in the elevator, I pushed her against the wall and started kissing her neck.

"You are insatiable." It wasn't a complaint as her hands gripped my shoulders and pulled me closer instead of pushing me away.

"Only for you," I agreed because it was the truth. I'd never been so enamored with anyone in my life.

The elevator doors opened, and I noticed Seline waiting in the lobby for Summer, just like she'd said. I spotted Caleb on the other side of her, trying to usher the guys onto the bus. Seline and Caleb had hit it off, no thanks to me and Summer crashing their first date.

Seline had been horrified at first when we walked toward their table, but when she saw how happy Caleb and I were to see each other, she forgave me and even let us hang around for the rest of dinner. But as soon as the meal was over, she kicked us to the curb—metaphorically— after saying some shit in French, most likely cursing us out and demanding we leave. Caleb moved here shortly after nailing his interview and getting hired on as staff. They'd been inseparable ever since.

"I'll see you at the field," I said before giving Summer a long kiss good-bye and smacking her on the ass.

Some girls shouted my name repeatedly, but I pretended like I didn't hear them. The truth was that I didn't give a fuck what they wanted. I had everything I needed.

I watched as Seline threw her arm around Summer's waist, and they watched us load onto the bus and eventually drive away. It made me feel calmer, knowing that Summer had her best friend traveling with her to the away games. She'd made a few good friends with the wives on the team, but they didn't travel all the time since most of them had kids. It seemed like all the women had their own things going on, so you never knew who was going to be at the game and who wasn't.

I hated whenever I had to leave her alone. I left for the stadium hours before the game even started, sometimes before she even woke up. It killed me, thinking how bored she must be even though she reassured me that she never was.

"I'm falling in love with that woman," Caleb said as he plopped down next to me and looked at our girls as they disappeared out of view.

"We all know."

"You ready for tonight?"

"Always."

"I mean, after," he whispered before patting his pocket.

"As long as you don't lose my fucking ring," I snapped.

I was going to propose to Summer in front of a packed stadium, on national television, after we won this game and secured our Super Bowl spot. Hell, I was going to propose to her even if we lost. But we weren't going to lose.

DIDN'T SEE THAT COMING

SUMMER

I WAS UNCHARACTERISTICALLY nervous for tonight's game, and I had no idea why. Of course, I wanted the team to go to the Super Bowl, but what happened if they lost tonight? Maybe that was why I was so rattled. I was unsure of how Crew would react to losing this far into the season. I knew how badly he wanted to go all the way, especially in his first season with the team.

"Have you made a decision about work yet?" Seline asked as we headed into the suite reserved for some of the players' significant others.

A couple of the girlfriends were there, each one wearing a sparkly jacket with her boyfriend's last name on it.

"We'll get you one, Summer," one of them said, and I

smiled.

"I'd like that. They're really cute."

Seline and I moved to a corner and sat down, our VIP passes dangling around our necks.

"So? Did you decide about work? Yes or no?"

I'd been slowly trying to figure out what to do, going forward with my company. I didn't want to continue working the way I had before Crew was in my life, but I also didn't see myself not working at all and giving it all up.

"Yeah, but I haven't told Crew yet."

"Why not?"

"I was just waiting until the season ended. I don't want him worrying about that stuff now, you know?" I said, and she nodded in agreement before pushing me for more information.

"You're not going to work like before, are you?"

I shook my head. "No. My plan is to work in the off-season only. Limit my time and take on shorter-term clients who won't need as much hand-holding. But nothing that will interfere with the football season. What about you?"

"What about me what?"

"Are you ever going to slow down?" I asked because Seline worked just as hard as I did. Sometimes harder with longer hours and even fewer days off.

"Not yet. I'm not where I want to be financially. But as soon as I hit that goal, I'll cut myself some slack," she said, and I understood her way of thinking completely. It felt good to be a successful woman with the ability to take care of herself.

I'd reached my financial goal years ago. It stopped being about the money then, and I'd mostly buried myself in work because I didn't have a personal life to speak of. It was easier to be busy all the time when you didn't have someone you wanted to share your days or nights with.

I didn't feel that way anymore. And there wasn't a single part of me that felt bad about my change of heart. Wanting to spend more time with Crew didn't make me any less successful. Having a partner to live life with didn't mean I wasn't independent. If anything, Crew made me feel more fulfilled, not less. He added to my every day; he didn't take anything away from it.

That was how I knew it was right. How he was my

person. And how pulling back from the business I'd started and created was an okay thing to do. Just thinking about it made me happy. I'd only looked forward to my career before. I was excited about life now.

THE GAME WAS a nail-biter, and we ended up winning by only a field goal. But it was enough to secure the team's spot in the Super Bowl, which was honestly more exciting than I'd thought it would be. When security arrived in the suite and asked all of us girls to come down onto the field, we happily obliged, each one of us giddy.

"We never go onto the other team's field," Seline whispered, and I nodded.

It was true. "I think this is a special occasion since they won. They're going to get a trophy for winning the division, and there will be speeches, yada, yada," I explained.

"American football is so odd." Seline waved me off, but even she couldn't hide the smile on her face.

As we neared the tunnel entrance to the field, Crew suddenly appeared, his dark hair all sweaty as strands of it fell near his eyes.

"I'll take this one," he said toward the security guard before focusing on me. "Hey, Duchess." He leaned down to give me a kiss. He was even taller in his cleats.

"Hey. How's it feel to be headed to the Super Bowl?" I asked, mimicking a reporter and using my fist as a fake microphone.

"Feels damn good." He grinned and reached for me with his free hand. His other hand was still holding his helmet. I wasn't sure if he even realized it or not.

"*Oh, hi, Seline. Nice to see you,*" Seline shouted from behind us as she followed us toward the group of hyped-up football players screaming and shouting over one another.

Caleb sauntered up to us and pulled Crew aside, an uncomfortable grin on his face as he cast us girls a weird look.

"What are they up to?" I asked, and Seline shrugged her shoulders, clearly as confused as I was.

After the temporary staging was set up on the field, someone tapped a microphone to get everyone's attention. The stands were still half-filled with fans. I noticed a reporter looking around, and I sensed that she was trying to find Crew. Everyone always wanted to interview the quarterback after a big win. But when I looked around, I couldn't find him either.

"Where did he go?" I asked Seline, whose expression was a mixture of surprise and shock. "What the hell is wrong with your face?"

She grabbed me by the shoulders and spun me around to where a small crowd had started forming behind me. I still had no idea what was going on, and then I looked down ... on the ground ... to where my gorgeous boyfriend sat on one knee, staring up at me. There was a glistening diamond ring between his fingers, no box in sight, and my stomach dropped.

"Summer," Crew started to say, and I sensed that we were being filmed by multiple people. I decided to focus only on him; otherwise, I might bolt. "Nothing in my life made sense until you walked into it. I never thought I'd find a partner, a teammate, or someone to share experiences with. Except for Bart, of course," he said, and I let out a small laugh. "The moment I met you, I knew. I know you'll argue and say that I couldn't have possibly known that day, but I did. And I've known every single day since that I want to be your husband. I want to make you proud. I want to fill you with babies. I want to spend the rest of my life making you happy. And I want to tell everyone in the world you're my wife and that I have no idea how I got so lucky."

I was crying, with no clue as to when it'd started, but full-on waterworks were leaving my eyes by that point.

"Will you marry me?" he finally asked, and I fell to my knees as I reached for him, my head nodding because my voice refused to work.

The cheers that broke out in the background were barely above a whisper to my ears; I was so lost in the moment and in this man. He reached for my left hand, which was shaking, and slid the ring in place before kissing me hard and long.

"I love you," he said as soon as he broke the kiss. "I can't believe you said yes."

"I love you too," I said before bringing my hand to my face so I could get a good look at the rock on my hand. It was ridiculous. But also perfect.

Just like my fiancé.

EPILOGUE

SUMMER

A YEAR LATER

CREW WAS WALKING around the house, naked. Again. With nothing but his championship Super Bowl ring on. It had become quite the routine for him—to flounce around with his big ole wiener out like it was no big deal.

"You're seriously naked right now?"

He stopped walking and thrust up his hand. "I have this on," he said with a proud smile. As if his ring counted as clothing.

"It's almost noon," I argued, like the time had any effect on Crew's nakedness. If the sun was out, his clothes were off.

"So? And you're one to talk. You're always wearing nothing, except that diamond." He pointed toward my left hand.

I gasped at the accusation. "You always make me take everything off, except this diamond." I imitated his tone and put my hand in the air too.

It was true though. Ever since Crew had put the large rock on my left hand, he'd kept demanding I never get dressed, so he could remind me who I belonged to and whose wife I was about to be. I always pretended to be annoyed, but I wasn't.

Not in the least.

But him walking around with nothing on all the time was starting to be a problem. Mostly because his body was one hell of a distraction and I was actually trying to work. Well, not *work*, work. But planning our wedding felt like a full-time job. Even with the wedding planner I'd hired, I was still bombarded by her requests and nonstop questions, followed by paperwork that always needed to be signed right away.

To be honest, I was a little too OCD to give up all the control to her anyway, so I was sure I was making things harder than they needed to be. But I only planned on doing this one time and never again. I wanted it to be perfect.

Our actual wedding date was still six months away, but it seemed like the details were never-ending. Everything needed to be booked yesterday with deposits paid and backup locations secured, just in case. The fires in SoCal had really altered the wedding industry. Not only did beautiful locations go up in flames without warning, but the remaining ones were overbooked and overpriced as well.

"Will you put some clothes on before they get here?" I tossed over my shoulder at my still-naked fiancé, who stood, looking out the window with a coffee mug in his hand. "You'd better hope no one sees you."

He turned to face me, his green eyes deep and heady. "*You'd* better hope no one sees me. They'll be lining up out the door, Duchess."

"Like they don't already," I said, rolling my eyes.

Crew had always been popular, but his line with Under Armour had introduced him to a whole new audience ... of younger females. For the most part, our house did a good job at keeping fans away, but there had been a few occasions where the gutsier girls rang our gate bell or tried to climb the fences to get inside.

Thankfully, that kind of stuff was rare and didn't happen often. The guys, pretended to be walking around the neighborhood. Sometimes, they even brought their dog, all hoping for a chance encounter with Crew. It was always obvious that they just wanted to meet him and didn't really live in the area, but Crew never called them out and was usually gracious.

The only time he'd ever lost his temper was when a man beelined straight past Crew and right toward me. I hadn't expected that as I stood there with Bart's leash in my hand. The man hadn't been there to meet Crew at all, which definitely caught us both off guard. I never assumed that anyone was purely there for Crew again. You just never knew.

When the security gate buzzed, I ran over to the system at the door and made sure it was who I thought before allowing them inside. Turning back around to yell at Crew, I noticed that he had already disappeared. Hopefully to put some actual clothes on.

I opened up the front door as soon as I saw the couple exit their car. They were beautiful to look at, like a walking ad for models. It shouldn't have surprised me, but it always seemed to. When I stepped outside to greet them, their faces lit up, and Bart ran outside behind me.

"Your house is stunning," the woman said as I tried to pull Bart back but failed.

"Thank you. We got really lucky. Sorry, this beast is Bart. Hi, I'm Summer," I introduced myself to them both as the man stepped around the car and stood next to his wife.

"I'm Robbie, and this is my wife, Jennifer."

I shook each of their hands before directing them inside.

"Thanks for coming to our house. I hope you don't feel like I was being unprofessional."

Right as we neared the front door, Crew appeared, fully dressed—thank God—as he called for Bart.

"Not at all." Robbie waved me off before adding, "Thank you for meeting us on a Saturday and for taking me on."

"I'm Crew Maxwell," Crew said as the couple walked into our home.

"I know who you are. That Super Bowl game last year was unbelievable, especially yourour pass in the third quarter. It's so nice to meet you."

The men shook hands and proceeded to get lost in some sort of sports talk that I swore only athletes could understand. It was like they were speaking a different language, and they talked so fast that I had no idea how they even kept up.

"I think we've lost them," Jennifer said, and I laughed as we neared the kitchen.

I reached for the pitcher of sun tea I'd made the other day and two glasses.

"We don't really need them anyway. Iced tea?" I asked, and she nodded.

It was true though. We both knew that Robbie would defer all of the home questions to his wife and most likely wouldn't make a big decision without her. That was how it usually went anyway. The women always made my job easier.

I'd cut back on work, like I'd planned on doing, and then I found myself not really missing it at all. When I'd gotten a call from my friend in the front office of our local hockey team, basically begging me to help out Robbie and his wife, I couldn't say no.

I still took on a handful of athletes, but it was growing fewer and further between them. Which was crazy, and before Crew, it would have been something that could never happen. Instead of wishing I were working when I wasn't, I got lost in creating travel bucket lists and sitting with Crew for hours, daydreaming about our future kids and our life.

I knew that, eventually, I was going to give up my work altogether in favor of raising our family and following our kids' dad around the country. And literally nothing made me happier than imagining that scenario.

Meeting Crew had changed my entire life and my outlook on it. I'd never known that I could feel so fulfilled from a personal relationship. I always thought that success and money were the things that filled up that proverbial jar. And in the past, they had been.

Not anymore.

I glanced up at Crew, who was staring at me from across the room. I watched as he put a finger in the air in Robbie's direction before stalking over toward me.

"I am so in awe of you. And I love you. And I can't wait to make you my wife," he announced as he neared me before grabbing the back of my neck and kissing me senseless.

I wanted to say something back … anything … but he kissed the words right out of me.

"Making me look bad, man," Robbie complained.

"Yeah, he is," Jennifer added, and I stood on wobbly knees, still staring at Crew.

That man was going to make one hell of a father and husband one day. And I couldn't wait to make him both.

The End

Thank you so much for reading my latest story in my Fun for the Holidays collection! I hope you enjoyed Summer & Crew's story as much as I did! It was a lot of fun to write and hopefully a lot of fun for you to read as well!

I came up with the idea for this series to give you all lighthearted and happy reads. But mostly, I just wanted you to enjoy yourself and get lost in a fictional world for a little while. I hope this story did that for you. And I hope all the rest will too!

Other Books by J. Sterling

Bitter Rivals – an enemies to lovers romance

Dear Heart, I Hate You

10 Years Later – A Second Chance Romance

In Dreams – a new adult college romance

Chance Encounters – a coming of age story

THE GAME SERIES

The Perfect Game – Book One

The Game Changer – Book Two

The Sweetest Game – Book Three

The Other Game (Dean Carter) – Book Four

THE PLAYBOY SERIAL

Avoiding the Playboy – Episode #1

Resisting the Playboy – Episode #2

Wanting the Playboy – Episode #3

THE CELEBRITY SERIES

Seeing Stars – Madison & Walker

Breaking Stars – Paige & Tatum

Losing Stars – Quinn & Ryson

About the Author

Jenn Sterling is a Southern California native who loves writing stories from the heart. Every story she tells has pieces of her truth in it as well as her life experience. She has her bachelor's degree in radio/TV/film and has worked in the entertainment industry the majority of her life.

Jenn loves hearing from her readers and can be found online at:

Blog & Website:

www.j-sterling.com

Twitter:

www.twitter.com/AuthorJSterling

Facebook:

www.facebook.com/AuthorJSterling

Instagram:

@ AuthorJSterling

Made in the USA
Coppell, TX
14 July 2022

79930972R10111